The Death of the Author

Gilbert Adair is the author of *Love and Death on Long Island*, *The Holy Innocents*, *Myths & Memories*, *Hollywood's Vietnam* and two sequels to children's literature, *Alice Through the Needle's Eye* and *Peter Pan and the Only Children.* A well-known journalist and broadcaster, he writes regular columns in the *Sunday Times* and *Esquire*.

Also by Gilbert Adair
and available in Minerva

The Holy Innocents
Love and Death on Long Island

GILBERT ADAIR

The Death of the Author

Minerva

A Minerva Paperback
THE DEATH OF THE AUTHOR

First published in Great Britain 1992
by William Heinemann Ltd
This Minerva edition published 1993
by Mandarin Paperbacks
an imprint of Reed Consumer Books Ltd
Michelin House, 81 Fulham Road, London SW3 6RB
and Auckland, Melbourne, Singapore and Toronto

Reprinted 1993

A CIP catalogue record for this title
is available from the British Library
ISBN 0 7493 9805 X

Printed and bound in Great Britain
by Cox & Wyman Ltd, Reading, Berks

Commit a crime, and the earth is made of glass. Commit a crime and it seems as if a coat of snow fell on the ground, such as reveals in the woods the track of every partridge and fox and squirrel and mole. You cannot recall the spoken word, you cannot wipe out the foot-track, you cannot draw up the ladder, so as to leave no inlet or clew.

Ralph Waldo Emerson

Since these mysteries are beyond us, let us pretend to have devised them.

Jean Cocteau

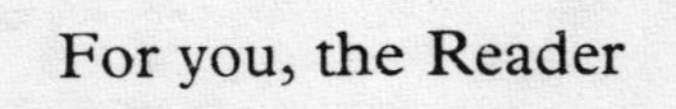
For you, the Reader

When she told me what it was she meant to do, my initial instinct was to look at my watch. This, merely a reflex on my part, an unfortunately timed one as I realized at once, she completely misunderstood. The smiling defiance tempered by apprehension with which she had announced her news to me swiftly drained from her features to be replaced by a moue of sulky disgruntlement. She was galled, nonplussed too, as I could see, that I had chosen no less than the crucial point in our interview, that at which she had played her trump card, to display what she presumably interpreted as my rude, fidgety impatience with her. Yet how could I convey to her that what I sought on my watch face was not the time but, as it were, time; that what I saw and all I saw (insofar as I saw anything at all) were the second and minute hands executing their immemorial hare-and-tortoise pursuit around the dial, the former advancing at a strictly measured pace, the latter, all wily invisible stealth, regularly outdistancing it from pit stop to pit stop? How was she to know that I had been waiting nearly seventeen years for someone to say to me what she had just said – for it, for this circumstance, to come about, as if it were finally its 'turn'? And how could I tell her that I had already made up my mind, possibly as late as at the very second she disclosed her project to me but already nevertheless, to forge ahead on my own? When things have to be said, they have to be said. Eventually they have to be said.

'Do I take it, Professor Sfax,' she asked in a tone suggesting that her previous temerity had once more got the upper hand, 'that your reservations –'

'Oh but, you see, I have no reservations,' I replied, smiling for the first time since my gaffe. 'On the contrary, I approve – for all that *that's* worth.'

Now she could barely credit how exorbitantly the situation seemed to have swung in her favor. 'So you won't, I mean to say, you won't put any obstacles in my way?'

I assured her I would lend every assistance that could reasonably be expected of me – I believe in diplomacy and, if occasion permit, tolerance – and would even compose a short preliminary text to aid her in her research. But I felt bound to warn her in the same breath that there was little enough I *could* do, that in particular most of the data relating to an earlier period of my life could no longer be appreciated or verified, too much of the relevant documentation having been lost. It was far too soon in any event to worry about all that. Understandably, she had preferred to speak to me first before even approaching a publishing house, and I may as well admit, although I naturally forbore to say so to her, that at this premature stage of its development the entire enterprise struck me as having a very moot future indeed.

It was as I accompanied her to my office door that I cast my famously mild eyes over her fair, bony, very patrician, very 'East Coast,' and altogether pretty face, fringed as by the pasteboard curtain sashes of a toy theater by a tangle of reddish-brown hair.

'You realize,' I said, smiling still, 'that you will never *get* me? Nobody ever has.'

Now it was her turn to smile, toothily, almost girlishly – a smile as spontaneous and unpremeditated as a blush.

'Didn't you know I sculpted?' she suddenly asked, as if it somehow 'showed,' for how I was otherwise supposed to know such a thing I couldn't imagine.

'No – really?'

'Only figurative stuff, I'm afraid. Heads, mostly. But they do say I'm very strong on likenesses. I mean to capture yours – if you'll let me.'

I made the primly strategic reply that first it would be for a publisher to let her – 'Where there's a will there's a way,' I murmured, '– or rather, where there's a way there's a will.'

She laughed; then, with a handshake, we said goodbye.

I returned to my desk to think over this strange little scene. I looked again at my watch, but this time just to see the time. Her appointment had been at five and it was by a minute gone half-past. So – it had taken only half-an-hour to cast the die. And it was a sculptress who cast it. A sculptress? Is everyone fated to have at least one sculptress in their life? Astrid! Her very name was a signifier of the 'creative' in all its poignant horror. No, truly no, I couldn't entrust my head to her.

I checked that I had no more appointments that afternoon and, satisfied that the rest of the day was mine to do with as I pleased, I switched on my Apple Mac computer. I opened a new file, to which I gave the password *Hermes*, and for a good five or six minutes sat there staring at the screen, the blank white screen-page, until at last I set to typing (I'm a two-finger man, basically – or even one, the left forefinger serving as not much more than the right's assistant, intervening, like the less agile half of a tennis doubles partnership, to bag an occasional comma or apostrophe) the four pages that you have just been reading.

I was born, an only child, in 1918, a very few weeks after the ceasefire, into a well-to-do, well-connected, and closely knit family with a Parisian town house in the Marais and a small property in the

Chevreuse valley, where our next-door neighbor, my father's dear friend, was Ravel no less. My childhood was happy and unhappy, normal and abnormal, outwardly quite uneventful, more or less inscrutable to hindsight, a bourgeois childhood in the Paris of the nineteen-twenties. My father was a publisher of fine-art books, and his father, after whom I was named, a minor and now mercifully forgotten poet and occasional librettist for Massenet.

It was at my grandfather's funeral that I suffered the first real hideous shock of my life. This was in 1931 and I was not quite thirteen, a proud little fellow, too, to be allowed to officiate as one of the pallbearers. The ceremony was being held in the tiny village that our Chevreuse house adjoined and that spring morning, under a gray sky, its square neat walled cemetery recalled one of those conventionally misty glades in which, at dawn's first crack, duels are fought by Hussars in imperial romances. I shed no tears during the service itself but when the coffin was undraped, about to be lowered into the earth, and I could see, engraved on a plaque on its lid, the name 'Léopold Sfax,' my grandfather's name, but no less (in fact peculiarly more so to my as yet savagely solipsistic view of the world) my own, I disgraced myself by giving way to a convulsive screaming fit and had to be led away by my Alsatian nurse, who sat me down on the hearse's running board, slapped my face once and hard, then rocked me – a thirteen-year-old boy – in her lap.

It was only much later that I learned to my great surprise – for I hadn't noticed what should have been flagrant enough even to an adolescent as reticent and bookish as I was – that, although not precisely 'not speaking' to one another, my father and grandfather had been estranged during almost the whole of the former's adult life.

The quarrel was partly a question of differences in matters of aesthetic taste. My grandfather had been the very last of the Parnassians, as his particular 'school' confidently styled itself, and his verse, written under the already withered sway of Théophile Gautier, was of a cold and glaucous classicism – the kind of dry studied thing a critic feeling chivalrous might call 'well-chiseled.' And it was as much on Parnassian principle as by his personal inclination that he let himself be infuriated at fairly regular intervals by the uncompromisingly modernist milieu in which my fascinated father moved, snorting at the Russian dancers and 'nigger' musicians whom he, my father, did indeed number among his acquaintances.

But there had also occurred a political falling-out that dated, insofar as my grandfather's engagement was concerned, from the last years of the last century. As was the rule in his stuffy out-of-favor clique, he had been an unflagging anti-Dreyfusard, and the natural, gradual, and so to speak chemical transformation of this hatred of the Jewish peoples into a mere drawing-room prejudice – a process that would certainly have taken place in due time – was forever thwarted by the fact that Zola himself, reviving his name only to murder his reputation, had attacked his stance in a published article of unforgettable and, by grandfather, long afterwards unforgotten viciousness and brio. Hence he was not so much an anti-Semite (in one of his letters he wrote that he might even have defended the wretched Captain out of simple humanity 'had he been worth the trouble') as an anti-'cosmopolitan,' standing fast against anything or anyone that threatened to contaminate the values of the good French soil. My father, for whom the term 'cosmopolitan' belonged in an esthetic rather than an ethnic category, lordlily refused for a second to indulge grandfather, though he was appreciably less high-minded, less of the purist, when speaking of his contacts with bankers and backers, in the world of bribes and rewards, and wasn't above taking nonchalant refuge in the unsavory euphemism 'Israelite' whenever he felt like it. So it was that we Sfaxes became a statistical unit: ours would be one of the thousands of families divided by the Dreyfus affair.

*

By the thirties, when I was mature enough to understand these issues, the Jewish question could no longer be left to personal conscience. I was in my first year of philosophy at the Ecole Normale Supérieure when, through the influence of my father, I started to publish in a small way in *Le Libre Arbitre*, a political monthly of insignificant circulation if not quite insignificant influence in which I naively endeavored to alert my becalmed and demoralized compatriots to the menace that loomed beyond our Eastern frontier.

These articles, and there were nine or ten at most, are probably lost beyond all recovering. Of them I recollect no more than random gleanings, and less any personal intuitions than a configuration, a common stock, of themes and lexicons that would be familiar to any student of the period's politics. I recall, for instance, that I flayed our Occidental civilization for its moral cowardice and decadence in the face of the horde of 'barbarians' who were now slavering at its gates. I emphasized the importance of a 'victory of the democracies' as the first necessary step toward the reestablishment of a social and political order the consideration of which would no longer fill us with shame or rage. I cited the urgent need for a framework of obligations and duties to which everyone would henceforth have to adapt their talents. And so forth. They were crudely programmatic, at best laconically polemic, but written with real ardor – ideas would come so fast to me I had to 'switch off' simply to put them into shape – and they possessed the virtue of being of their time and place, 'clever' work by a child of his own age.

I was twenty-one when the war came at last, twenty-two when my studies were interrupted, and possibly forever, as I felt it then, by the opening of a great valve that let a chill draft blow through the France I had been so fondly berating. No, not chill, hot: fear is cold, panic is hot. It had been the impending catastrophe that prompted my callow ambition as a journalist – it was its reality that brought it, and the series of poor little pieces, so facilely prophetic, which I had written for *Le Libre Arbitre*, to a quick and panicky end.

In the spring of 1940, when the Germans were closing in on the capital, my parents, myself, our chauffeur, and his pregnant wife piled the trunk of our automobile with the very best that could be saved of my father's collection of paintings, a goodish Matisse odalisque, a Braque, a pretty Harlequin by Derain, and fled a city that I already thought of as posthumous, driving south or southwest, anywhere the invader could not or would not follow us, joining a mazy meandering caravan of cars and trucks and jalopies and horsecarts, mattresses, cribs, chairs, tables, standard lamps, cardboard suitcases, famished dogs, and, naturally, the bizarre totem of the refugee, the family birdcage.

That same July we found cramped lodgings in a farmhouse in the area of Pau and tried throughout the month, tried repeatedly, to cross the frontier into Spain, whence we might reach Lisbon and the very rim of Europe, beyond which beckoned the Atlantic and the multifarious haven of America. But because too many fugitives were straining to squeeze through too narrow a neck in the bottle, because the frontier was being closed and opened and opened and closed with no discernible rhyme or reason on the part of the unseen authorities on both sides, and doubtless too because of our dawning apprehension of the awful plight we had gotten ourselves into, destined to live from then on and for who knew how long or for that matter where as refugees, history's poor relations, obliged before very many months had passed to sell off, at some shyster's take-it-or-leave-it price, the works of art we had fled precisely to preserve, my father took the decision to return to the capital to see if anything of our lives could still be salvaged from the disaster.

The house near the place des Vosges was as it had been left. Nothing was gone, or had been stolen, or defiled. Had we departed on a vacation it would not have looked any too different. Certainly, the servants having presumably also taken flight, the rooms were untidy and unaired, but through the efforts of our chauffeur and his wife everything was soon, so to speak, as good as old. The whole experience, an experience that had seemed so traumatic and life-transfiguring while it was happening, turned out to have been merely a parenthesis in our existence, open – then closed.

For me, as for all of us, the four years which followed were grim and joyless ones. I did resume my discontinued studies, but I ceased to publish articles, either in a political or more strictly literary vein, the former as there no longer existed a forum of opinion for anyone who would not espouse the New Order or did not cynically see advantage in marching to its tune, the latter as it would have made a mockery of a world which had lost whatever belief it once claimed to have in the civilizing power of the word. In 1942 or thereabouts I *was* invited to contribute to the collaborationist rag *Je suis partout* by Alain Laubreaux, a distant friend of my father, who was pleased to recall to me what he called the modest excellence of my prewar writings – an awkward situation from which I fancy I extricated myself with a fair degree of elegance. (A thoroughgoing collaborator himself, and well aware that I could scarcely have written openly for so very disreputable a publication, he proposed with repulsive delicacy that I adopt a pseudonym.) And talking of my father I must now mention the single most shaming fact of my youth: his progressive, not collaboration with – rather, accommodation to the Germans.

My father was, it should be said, far from alone in surrendering to the gross moral laxness of such a gentleman's agreement between the occupier and the occupied. By the middle of the war the capital could barely be distinguished from the amusing, oppressive epicenter of all the world's gaiety and charm that it had been before the occupier's arrival. Cafés, restaurants, theaters, movie theaters, and nightclubs had reopened, their best places tending to be 'occupied' by the stylish and respectable element of the German High Command; and as long as enough of this public's hands were heard to be clapping, actors and actresses seemed little to care whose blood might still be fresh on them.

Yet far more sickening to me than the easy slumming fraternization of sophisticates was the flimsy set of rationalizations by which the less witless of them hoped to acquit themselves of their misbehavior. Dining with Nazis only the better to help one's Jewish friends at risk of deportation was one such; sanctioning performances of one's work only to avert the definitive snuffing out of French culture another favorite. Others may have been duped, but I was close enough to my father to know that the nature of *his* clubby fellowship with the higher-rank-ing type of German was one of pure professional opportunism. His publishing business having foundered for want of the fine paper and bindings his books had been famous for, he had become, without any of us observing the precise moment of transition, an art dealer, specializing in the contemporary Ecole de Paris and increasingly finding that his most promising clients were 'nice' sorts of Germans, francophile dignitaries attached to the Embassy and the Franco-German Institute. (He even succeeded in selling a couple of paintings on the sly to Otto Abetz himself, the ambassador.) It wasn't just the indefensible indecency, as it struck me, of his being so thick with torturers and killers (men who, speaking in public, would denounce as 'decadent,' as the root cause of France's fall, the selfsame artists whose work they were snapping up in private) that turned my stomach. It was also the anxiety on my part, an anxiety never assuaged by my slippery father, concerning the exact provenance of these paintings that were suddenly his to sell, an anxiety at its acutest whenever I happened to wander through the atelier in our house where the canvases were stored and my gaze fixed upon the little yellow paper circles stuck to the frames of those already sold but still to be delivered. But I never did learn, and to this hour do not know, how my father came by them.

*

I left home in the fall of that year of 1942 to move in with a law student friend of mine, Paul, and his girlfriend Louise, who shared a minute cluttered unruly apartment on the Ile Saint-Louis. It was mostly off my money that we three survived – I had a paltry, devalued, but still unspent legacy from my grandfather – and fairly thrived on macaroni and broth. And it was there that I continued to live until the Liberation, at first with both friends, then, following Paul's disappearance, with Louise alone.

I confess to a faint aversion, even now, to speaking of this period of my life. I realize that modesty is a secretly despised virtue, resented by all those whom another man's modesty is destined to make look vain. Modest I have to be all the same, since my patchy and insignificant contribution to the struggle couldn't honestly be described any more elevatedly.

From one of the libraries that I frequented I returned late one afternoon to the Ile Saint-Louis to find a clandestine-looking meeting just breaking up in the apartment. I had it out with Paul, and when I learned the truth begged him to allow me to join his 'cell.' Slightly to my amazement, though, I was to discover that the Resistance, the true, was a wonderfully exclusive organization, insanely particular as to who ought to be permitted to bear arms in its name. Yet, if hesitant at first, and convinced that his comrades would turn me down flat, Paul was eventually persuaded to speak on my behalf, and in the next two years I did what I could and what they allowed me to do. Let it be left at that.

Otherwise I read greedily and, there too, clandestinely. My author of the hour was Hegel, in tandem with Alexandre Kojève's incomparable exegesis, a premature taste at a time when the great philosopher was, even to those few countrymen of mine who had heard of him at all, just another Boche. And I would take Louise out once or twice a week to catch any old and bad movie provided it was what is called 'escapist.' These movies were indispensable to our well-being, our only means of escaping, vicariously as it had to be, from the Nazis.

In the August of 1944 Paris's German garrison capitulated to the Allies and a year later the war was over. The Europe it left behind was a terrifying if also an oddly liberating *tabula rasa*, whose ghoulishly picturesque ruins would be picked over, paid visit to, by our cheerful chocolate-, gum-, and cigarette-bearing liberators as if they had been preserved, like so many jerry-built (or perhaps one should say jerry-destroyed) Parthenons, solely for their delectation.

That my father had seriously compromised himself during the war was evident and he was duly hauled before one of the committees of the *épuration*. Yet because he was less culpable than I had long tended to suspect or simply because he was too small a fish, when downright monsters were being landed almost every day, not to be contemptuously cast back into his fetid little pond, his condemnation was a merely verbal one. I certainly didn't grudge him that, but I'd passed my own judgment on his offense, a judgment that nothing in this public mitigation of its magnitude caused me to revise. In any case I ceased to see very much of him from that point (he would mainly stay put in the house in the Chevreuse Valley, prematurely old and broken by his disgrace) until my eventual departure for the United States. He died in 1951, when I would willingly have returned to pay a last tribute to him in the same cemetery in which my grandfather had been buried, but I was desperately short of funds and felt that it would have been cowardly to impose upon my mother, whose own material insecurity in such hard times I could well imagine.

So it was that I emigrated to America in 1949 after four useless restless languid years when I lazed about and took my *agrégation* in philosophy and privately set to turning myself, precisely in anticipation of the voyage I knew I had to make, into a fluent English speaker (although the then fashionable English authors whom I read for the purpose, Meredith and du Maurier and Charles Morgan, and who forever marked my own oral and written manner in that tongue, would ill equip me for the elastic, eclectic vernacular of my adopted country). Europe had nothing to offer me now, all the more so in that, a few months before my departure, having spent a long weekend at my parents' house in the country, to visit my mother, I came home to find that Louise had gone, apparently for good – but *that* I had seen coming – and had removed from the apartment, as an electrically terse little message informed me, only what she said she knew to have been hers and Paul's.

No matter how, later, my feelings about America were to be qualified by exposure at firsthand to its ways, I own that in that sandy-lidded dawn when, like hundreds of my fellow steerage passengers, I scrambled onto the ship's deck to gawp at New York's façade of skyscraping cigarette-lighters and paperweights, I thought it quite sheerly irresistible. The prospect, as well, that once I had undergone the, as it turned out, not especially demeaning immigration process I would actually emerge at the other, the far side of the façade, would be stepping out onto the fabled soil, walking *between* those rows and rows of skyscrapers, I still regard as one of the most exalting I've ever known.

I had a few dollars, no friends, and just one connection, a former Jewish acquaintance of my father who had emigrated to the States in the late thirties and managed one of the small good quiet bookstores in Greenwich Village. Raphaël was to be my very first friend in America, my first employer, too, and his own and his wife's friends soon became mine, émigrés all of them – exile has its own language and its own nationalism: expatriates are compatriots – all of them, too, intellectuals in their way. For some few years thereafter I toiled obscurely in Raphaël's store, occupying, sometimes alone, sometimes with a companion, an underfurnished two-room apartment on Eighth Street. Before America discovered me, before, in a sense, it ever knew that I existed (except insofar as all of us immigrants secretly believed that America like God had an occult awareness of every last one of its creatures), I discovered it, and found nothing so low or mean that it could not be ennobled by my immigrant's gaze. I was happy and industrious and frequently, if seldom lastingly, in love.

On Sunday afternoons Raphaël and his wife entertained in a back room of the store. There were also readings there on occasion, in the sympathetically Greenwich Villagey mode, by bad poets who would afterwards, over coffee and cookies, turn out to be perfectly nice people, not at all stupid. I myself was asked to contribute a paper, on which I worked so hard and so long, to the sole end of getting the English right, that without realizing quite what I was doing I made of it meanwhile a more highly-wrought thing than I'd really intended it to be.

Its subject was Mallarmé's *L'Après-midi d'un faune* and it elaborated a somewhat fantastical thesis on the poet's queer choice of the word 'afternoon' in his title, an afternoon being a specifically modern division of time, thus entering into collision with the conventional landscape and mindscape of the eroticized classical mythology that the poem inhabits – a thesis, in short, on the wilful incongruity of fauns and nymphs disporting, not in the morning or at night, dawn, or dusk, all eligibly 'classical' times of day, but in the gossipy tea-taking afternoon. In this anachronism (as I proposed) lay not simply a distinctively Mallarméan preciosity but the very model of an already ironically laced modernity which, many years later, I would come to comprehend as a precocious postmodernism. That at any rate was my basic *propos*; and even if Mallarmé's verse was scarcely all the rage, and couldn't have been further removed from the rowdy Whitmanesque ravings that I'd had to put up with from the circle of Sunday poets, my paper went down well – I actually noted one or two of my audience visibly 'mulling over' what I had just said. And by a glorious chance – and rather like, in the sort of corny movie musicals I had a weakness for in those days, a Ziegfeld talent scout dropping in on some amateur barnyard revue and instantly signing up its ingénue – there happened to come to that particular gathering the editor of an influential literary journal, who promised to publish the paper if I would suitably revise and abridge it.

I found myself 'taken up.' By that editor, and through the interest aroused by that first and the several ensuing essays that I contributed to his journal, I was presented to Harry Levin, to Mary McCarthy and Edmund Wilson, all of whom professed real enthusiasm for what I didn't yet dare to affect to regard as my 'work' but which I increasingly dared to hope might become my vocation.

It wasn't that I was exactly eager to leave the bookstore in which I labored uncomplainingly and which, if it was in its material dimensions small and to some might have seemed claustrophobic, was made huge for the chronic browser that I was by the compacted immensities of literature. But it had certainly never been my intention not to move on, and if I read widely during my stay there I also read systematically, so that when these new champions of mine got together to help me better myself and Wilson wrote a generous letter to the head of the small Comparative Literature department at Breen, an undistinguished northwestern college, who offered me a first and modest enough teaching post, I felt sufficiently confident of my abilities and qualifications, equally confident of having by then met all my obligations to Raphaël and his wife, as to have absolutely no hesitation in accepting.

Initially, no doubt, I was even a whit overconfident: at this, the inceptive phase of my bright new career, I fear my performance as a lecturer left rather a lot to be desired. Indeed, although I more than got by on my salary, I was so apprehensive of being dismissed sooner or later that I resolved to cover myself by privately tutoring a group of clucking local matrons (who were above all enamored, as I had cause to know, of my accent and general suavity) in both French and German and moonlighted one balmy summer as an usher in a movie theater.

Nothing was to come to me with ease. But I did grow into the job as first months then years passed, my contented cloistered bachelor's existence paced by the regular blink of turning book pages, and I cautiously began to make a name for myself as a critic, articles of mine appearing in not only a number of scholarly journals but also in the very best of the nonacademic intellectual press, notably the book pages of the *New York Times*.

I taught for two years at Amherst; then, in the mid-sixties, my reputation was already such that, while working on my graduate thesis, I was granted a threc-year post at Cornell, with relatively few teaching responsibilities, a decent salary at last, and the opportunity to familiarize myself at close hand with the 'New Criticism' that was the current orthodoxy in English departments. Although the essays I was writing were judged to be of unusual brilliance and depth, and were much photocopied on campus, I had my reasons for resisting demands that they be collected in a single volume, and it wasn't until 1972, a whole two years after being appointed to a professorship at New Harbor – I was apparently now a 'catch' in the academic star-system – that I published my first book, a study of Yeats.

That book, whose appearance produced quite a commotion, I may even say a scandal, in the advanced academic circles of the day, was *Either/Either* – I realized I had 'arrived' when the *Partisan Review* reviewer wrote of it as having been wildly overrated, for to be described as overrated by one critic meant after all that I had been highly rated by several.

As its title was to become the object of some good-natured ribbing from my colleagues, just as to how it had to be pronounced, and briefly 'entered the language,' being picked up by *Newsweek* and the *Village Voice*, I sat myself down at the Faculty Club's rickety upright on one destined-to-be-legendary evening, an event actually reported in the *New Harbor Advocate*, the local free rag, and offered the definitive, puckishly musical explanation. To the tune of 'Let's Call the Whole Thing Off,' amateurishly picked out on the just about serviceable piano,

I sang in a light baritone voice and, I fear, faintly Maurice Chevalierish accent:

> 'You say eyether and I say eeether,
> You say writer and I say reader,
> Eyether – eeether,
> Writer – reader,
> Let's call the whole thing off.'

There were several more verses in the same vein, half-improvised doggerel involving Yeats and Keats, Maud Gonne and John Donne – but the session was a personal triumph and I believe is talked about still.

It was, you will recall, the very heyday of the death of the Author and the correlative rise of the Reader as the text's interpreter, its sole and lonely arbiter. These ideas had come to us from Paris, as so many had before, and they had until then been merely spooned out, in a wary and parsimonious trickle, to the academic community of my adopted homeland. So that the central premise of my book – to wit, *Who cares what Yeats meant? His poems mean* – my insistence, just as my fellow critics were straining to isolate *the* interpretation, that literary meanings were generated not by their nominal author but from an accumulation of linguistic conventions and codes, and my categorical refusal to regard documented authorial intentions as a privileged source of information on the work under study were all still capable of roiling the placid, stagnant pools in the ornamental gardens of academe.

But such once radical views have become critical commonplaces now, even in America, and so grossly simplified an account of them will risk exasperating the informed reader while continuing to baffle the uninitiated. Suffice it to say that, if the reception of *Either/Either* was naturally very gratifying to me, its premises remained to my then way of thinking too subservient to certain, particularly French, models to be totally satisfying.

It was the book that followed it, by two years, that altered my entire existence. This, entitled *The Vicious Spiral*, as no one will need to be reminded, was a collection of essays that made me by far the most celebrated critic in the United States and New Harbor a point of convergence for all that was novel and creative and advanced in my field. And although I myself had modestly resisted labeling as a 'theory' the project on which I had embarked, nothing could have been more futile. For, precisely because of my aversion to naming it, it – 'it' – was to attain notoriety in virtually every campus in the country, in every department at least of English or Comparative Literature, as simply, baldly, the Theory. The Theory!

If I had realized how it would 'take,' how it would engulf the small tight inbred universe of literary studies, just how many reputations it would be held responsible for making and also breaking, I dare say, sincerely, that I might have decided against publishing the thing at all. But perhaps I ought to have known what would happen. The sensation which my book caused had been preceded the year before by the publication of a work by my friend Harold Bloom, *The Anxiety of Influence*, whose brilliant and interesting preoccupation it was that influence among writers constituted no benevolent, mutually congenial relaying of the torch from the cherished master to the cherishing disciple; that by contrast those disciples who come after, and inherit the laws and lessons of the master, are obsessed by their lateness on the scene, are Oedipally haunted by forerunners whom they obscurely resent for having 'queered their pitch,' as they say, and whom they are committed to misread, against the traditional timeworn interpretative grain, if ever they are to find a place for themselves in the sun. I thought highly of Bloom's book, and indeed wrote a very laudatory notice of it in *The Times Literary Supplement*, but privately cared little for the pathos of his concept of 'anxiety.' Bloom, I liked to quip, had confused influence with influenza and novels with navels.

Where he and I coincided nevertheless was in our shared belief in the unpreventability of texts being thus 'misread.' What was new and, dare I say, explosive in *The Vicious Spiral*, in the Theory, was its exposition of the utter and terminal insecurity of absolutely every such 'reading'; and in a passage destined to become infamous I refused to confine these readings to a purely literary framework but proposed innumerable other categories of experience whose meaning was no less a function of interpretation – social conditions, wars, even death – as so many 'texts.' The more closely a text is studied the more insidiously is it drained of sense or legibility, just as the more fixedly a word is stared at on the page the more too is it drained of legibility or sense, striking the increasingly bewildered eye as a mere weird disconnected sequence of squiggles. Words are far older and fickler and more experienced than the writers who suffer under the delusion that they are 'using' them. Words *have been around.* No one owns them, no one can prescribe how they ought to be read, and most certainly not their author. Consequently, as I endeavored to show, and *did* show, if the numbers of my followers and the fanaticism of their devotion to my cause constitute any kind of firm evidence, the literary text cannot help but undermine itself and *a fortiori* its author's 'intentions'; it will always go its own way, generate its own free play of unprivileged, unsecured, and frequently contradictory interpretations; and the written language will therefore always contain within itself the possibility of affirming mutually exclusive meanings: neither either/or nor neither/nor but either/either.

So it was, with the advent of the Theory, that the Author was to find Himself declared well and truly dead. Since I had demonstrated that it was for language to do the thinking, for the text to 'write' its author rather than vice versa, the presence of a human sensibility somehow embedded within that language, within that text, had at last been understood for what it truly was: an absence, a void. The old and handy pedagogical dichotomies, the so-called binary oppositions that had once served to authenticate the truth and completeness of the Author's interior universe – identity and difference, nature and culture, self and society – had at last been reversed or dissolved. 'Meaning' itself had lost its centrality in an infinitely extensible network of associated ideas. What had always been interpreted as central to a text was abruptly rendered peripheral, indeed all but irrelevant; which in its own turn had on the motivated reader the intoxicating effect of his discovering that every text would tend to say something completely other than what it 'meant to say.' Or 'say' nothing at all. For, in the single most clangorous note of defiance struck by *The Vicious Spiral* against all the venerable lit. crit. verities, I proposed that, again in *every* text, there would fatally arrive what I called an *aporia*, a terminal impasse, a blank brick wall of impenetrability, an ultimatum of indetermination, when its self-contradictory meanings could no longer be permitted to coexist in harmony and its fundamental 'undecidability' would undermine for ever the reader's most fundamental presuppositions.

It was, as it happens, at that last proposition that the long-suffering scoffers at the Theory were determined to *draw the line* – rather, it was by the window of opportunity offered by its theoretical incontinence and by the enormity of its affront to sheer common sense that they sought to infiltrate and invade the rest of the fortress. What? they squealed from Berkeley to Brown, and from Wesleyan to Columbia, is nothing to mean anything any more? *Hamlet*, *Faust*, *Moby-Dick*, *The Divine Comedy* – that these possess not one meaning, fair enough, but are they then to possess so very many that it becomes meaningless for the reader to explore any of them? To which the screw-turners, nostrils twitching at the whiff of sulphur, would add: And Auschwitz? Dresden? Hiroshima? My Lai? All of them meaningless, indecipherable texts, saying the opposite of what we had always imagined they said? Wars as texts – go tell that, they protested, to the Marines, go tell that to the maimed, gassed, blinded, disfigured victims of civil texts and guerilla texts and one day, doubtless, the great nuclear text.

For the most part these assaults on my book, which neither told nor bit deep, remained quite unwounding, founded as they were on the emotional futilities and sentimental vulgarities of precisely the old and exhausted humanism to which *The Vicious Spiral* stood in such stark contradiction. That reactionary elements in New Harbor and elsewhere would feel threatened by my theories I knew long before they themselves had time to formulate their objections. That they would balk at this aporetic cul-de-sac which, in the tongue-twisting words of one hostile critic, rendered all texts 'inextinguishably and indistinguishably incomprehensible' I could certainly have divined in advance. That they would take exception, take violent exception, to my perhaps after all ill-judged pronouncement that 'death is a displaced name for a linguistic predicament' I had well prepared myself for. What I had *not* prepared myself for was the implacable passion, the intransigence under fire, and not least the sheer numbers of my disciples. Strengthened from within by the very obduracy of those who elected to range themselves against it, the victory of the Theory was instantaneous and total. Its intellectual conviction and self-sufficiency, its iconoclasm and rarefaction, its bold fundamentalist capacity to exhilarate the adherent and shock the opponent, its terrible democracy – how these would be pounced upon by scholars who craved only to surrender to the cold voluptuousness of negativity. The world had been turned upside-down – what had always been true was false, what had been important was marginal, what had been meaningful was meaningless – and it made sense, it made sense!

Alas, it was all, I fear, where too many of these converts were concerned, a question not of rationality but of faith, of epiphany – of *seeing the light*. One minute they were perplexed, they were outraged – the next minute they actually knew what I was talking about. They had become Theorists.

Like Byron I woke up a national glory. The big galumphing world of letters discovered me, and I was proclaimed, and anointed, and crowned. Along the leafy, beigy-green, as though permanently autumnal, streets of New Harbor, in the shadow of the twisting primary-hued Calder mobiles on the forecourt of the Ruggles Library, I would walk between watching faces and envious murmurs, my colleagues and students alike acknowledging by a nearly intangible suppletion of respect and curiosity the high lonesomeness of unbreathably pure theory. As I had always done, in the morning, on my way to a class or to the Ruggles, I would cross the City Burial Ground, entering it by the arched mock-medieval gateway that read 'The Dead Shall Be Raised' and sharing its tranquil matinal morbidity only with the gray squirrels that perched on the tombstones, little balls of fur and fear among the choir invisible. Now, such was my frighteningly sudden fame, even the dead seemed to be whispering of it to one another, to be debating the Theory and its potential applicability to their condition.

There was a perceptible transformation, too, in my material circumstances. The 'catch' could not be permitted now to escape – although as it happens this 'catch' had no intention of leaving. I was too happy at New Harbor, I felt that with my new-found albeit not wholly sought-for eminence as the pope of the Theory I was the best of all possible things in the best of all possible worlds, a big fish in a big pond. I did, to be sure, receive delicately worded communications from heads of rival Comp. Lit. departments, once or twice from their Deans, proposing, should I care to make the move, to reward me with a chair, a graduate program, an inexhaustible series of research grants, as many sab-baticals as I could handle, and an office with its bathroom and even bedroom *en suite*. I tried to be fairly discreet about these proposals – to Donleavy, an Irish-born colleague who was pathologically pre-occupied with the politics of 'headhunting' and who would greet me in the Tudor Club gym with a 'Well, well, if it isn't Leo' – his tone dropping at once to a sly sidelong whisper – 'tell me, old man, you been poached lately?' I would reply only with a crinkly smile that could have meant anything he wished to make it mean. Yet, as months passed, and long after the subsidence of that interest that the

Theory and I had once aroused among the media mafia, I discovered that many of the same academic frills and filigrees were mine for the asking at New Harbor. I was suddenly offered a new light roomy office that overlooked the green-and-gravel grounds of the Alumni House and gave me easy access to a pool of departmental secretaries: it didn't have its own bedroom but it did have a kind of cozy closety denlike annex with a fair-sized couch that could be snoozed if not quite slept on. And I found myself gradually eased out of all the more onerous of departmental duties, those that would have entailed my serving on committees of one type or other, and free to patronize the several conferences that were being held around the country on my work and eventually, I was led to understand, to hole up if I wanted to and for as long as I wanted to in Connecticut or on the Cape and produce another *Vicious Spiral* – who knows, a better mousetrap of a Theory.

Insofar as any so starchily ethereal pursuit could be, the Theory had become fashionable and I with it. I was thankful, though, that its modishness in this respect did not equally imply any intensification of my all but nonexistent public life. I was probably regarded as too unattainable, too far beyond the ruck, just too hair-raisingly hermetic a thinker, to be interviewed by *Time* or the *New York Times*, the ungrateful mission of vulgarization being left to my more personable and articulate disciples. That at any rate is how it was supposed to have worked. Yet, oddly enough, those volumes that were brought out in the wake of mine, and whose publicly declared intention it was to supply a gloss on it – I think of Ethan Darwell's *About the Theory*, Sarah Everett's *Criticism in Crisis*, my friend Saïda's *Saint-Trope*, and, from England, perhaps surprisingly, de'Ath's *The Gentrification of the Void* – struck me as very much more unreadably rebarbative than anything I myself had written in *The Vicious Spiral.*

As a critic and theorist I do, as I am aware, pose problems enough, but only because the concepts I manipulate are problematic in and of themselves. I flatter myself, however, that I have succeeded in retaining a quite heroic clarity of expression in the face of those temptations which the Theory's disciples, many of whom seem to get a thrill from simply jangling the small change of its lexicon, have found irresistible. I have never felt the need, for *example*, to *abuse* the pedal of *italics*. I do not regard 'it' as a loss of my theorist's 'face' if I should decline to distance myself from the rhetorically 'bequeathed' properties of 'a' word by festooning it with a sweet little flight of quotation marks like plaster geese over a mantelpiece. It has not occurred to me to seek to enlarge/refine the significance/resonance produced by my writing by splitting every other word with a virgule/slash mark. Or scar the text with a visible erasure as a ~~symbol~~ of the polysemous ambiguity of all discourse. So abstruse but also so important, I believed, was what I wished to say, I was resolved to keep it as free as humanly possible of jargon, for which in any event I have an almost intestinal distaste.

Nor am I so modest as to seek to deny that the fashionableness of the Theory, as also the initial absence of animosity toward me personally among its several declared and vocal opponents, was in no small part a legacy of my own charm and wit. There is bound to be, I know, something suspect about a first-person account of charm, an admission to which, from the bearer himself, must seem to go some way to negating the very quality it advertises. Yet I cannot pretend to have remained unaware of the effect on others of, in my personal bearing, a rare admixture of the accommodating and the aloof, of new-world self-application and good old-fashioned, old-world world-weariness, a cocktail of qualities that could be relied upon to vanquish doubters and rout detractors and would prove particularly seductive to my feminine students. I bore my genius lightly, was the consensus.

Astrid Hunneker was one student on whom that circean charm had a luridly pronounced effect. Not even the blurry expanses of a packed auditorium would prevent my eyes from establishing instantaneous contact with her intense scrutiny of me.

She had come, a flickeringly brilliant if too conventionally focused student, from Mount Holyoke, to write her graduate thesis at New Harbor, and had chosen as her director, without it seems heeding her friends' appeals or her own ponderations, Herbert Gillingwater. Gillingwater, I should explain, to convey a rough idea of what the Theory was ruthlessly weeding out of sight if not yet of existence, was one of the university's oldest troupers, a mediocre, almost unpublished journeyman-scholar who had given his course on Culture and Society since the year dot. He was a kind of Peter Pan in reverse, never known to have been young. Indeed, his mousy nicotine-stained moustache and frankly sepia beard impressed one as older even than he was, deeply unappetizing hand-me-downs from some ancient parent; and it was claimed of him, an old maid of a bachelor, that if the striation of the corduroy suit he wore in all weathers looked as raggedly corrugated as it did, it was that he would freshen it simply by plunging it every six months or so into a sinkful of boiling water and detergent. Yet, lost cause as he was, hopeless anachronism as he struck the purest practitioners of the Theory, he was an individual beloved, the very nicest man, it was said, on the campus. Wholly without ambition, he was no less without enemies. It was as hard to dislike him as it was to admire his 'mind.'

I had once or twice publicly humiliated him without really meaning to. I remember an evening in the Faculty Club dining room after a guest lecture from David Lodge, the British critic and novelist. Apropos of something harmlessly murmured by Lodge over the coffee cups, Gillingwater, in his own cups, had started to expatiate on Keats' 'Ode to a Nightingale,' reciting it aloud with an actor-managerish extravagance of expression and making a real meal, in his characteristically moth-eaten manner, of what he saw as the unmatched pathos of the poet's repetition of the word 'forlorn' in the two concluding stanzas:

'Thou wast not born for death, immortal Bird!
No hungry generations tread thee down;
The voice I hear this passing night was heard
In ancient days by emperor and clown;
Perhaps the self-same song that found a path
Through the sad heart of Ruth,
When, sick for home,
She stood in tears amid the alien corn;
The same that oft-times hath
Charm'd magic casements, opening on the foam
Of perilous seas, in faery lands forlorn.

'Forlorn! the very word is like a bell

To toll me back from thee to my sole self!
Adieu! the fancy cannot cheat so well
As she is fam'd to do, deceiving elf.
Adieu! adieu! thy plaintive anthem fades
Past the near meadows, over the still stream,
Up the hill-side; and now 'tis buried deep
In the next valley-glades:
Was it a vision, or a waking dream?
Fled is that music: – Do I wake or sleep?'

We listened to this stuff in an embarrassment – Lodge's, I imagine, being especially acute – so excruciating it might have been mistaken for emotion, and into the silence that followed, and that poor blest Gillingwater visibly deluded himself had been prompted by the pressing need for a moment of awestruck rumination all round, I dropped this comment: 'You know, Herbert, "forlorn" has always sounded like "foghorn" to me.'

It was typical of his ineradicable lovability (which didn't deserve to be grilled as severely and frequently as it was) that, after a second or two when it looked as if he might burst into tears, the tensions knotting his hurt and hapless features abruptly relaxed and he was the first to laugh.

From that evening on Gillingwater became something of a Boswell of mine, as fascinated by my throwaway intuitions – which were often crushing to his own views of literature – as he was puzzled by instead of truly hostile to the intricacies of the theoretical work on which my prominence at large had been founded. What lingers in my mind is his eternally endearing 'Oh, come *on*, Leo...' of incredulity whenever I would give myself up to the bliss of that theory or gaily damn some writer, Nabokov, for example, to whose novels he was, as I thought it, inexplicably partial. When he championed Nabokov as 'a writer's writer,' and I countered smoothly (and not entirely impromptu, I have to confess) that if he was it was only in the sense in which the English refer to a valet as a gentleman's gentleman, he would return the ball to me with a trusty and inevitable 'Oh, come *on*, Leo...' (as my own accent disappeared, so did that on my Christian name), then fall about giggling as if it weren't simply the most outrageous but the wittiest slander he had ever heard. And when he repeated it, as he invariably would, it never occurred to him that the *mot* didn't necessarily depend, for its effect, on a context in which he was destined to play the patsy. It was so like Herb that he would always happily tell the story against himself.

In any event Gillingwater was Astrid Hunneker's director of thesis; and since that thesis, as I would subsequently learn, was a not altogether plausible feminist reading of *The Woman in White* which she had entitled 'Voice Bonding: the Gender of the Omniscient Author,' it was a role in which – as eventually dawned on both of them at once – he could not have been more miscast. What happened, as she was later to tell me, is that little in her experience at Mount Holyoke, one of the primmer of the Seven Sisters, which she treated as not much more than a finishing school, had trained her to engage with a febrile species of intellectual speculation of which New Harbor was then the unchallenged nursery. Brilliant and lazy, she had sought out Gillingwater through some vague notion that he would allow her to go her own wayward way, and had only very progressively arrived at the belated, the bitter realization that exciting, that *fashionable* things were taking place around her. Time and the Theory appeared to be passing her by and Herb scarcely was the man to guide her through the thickets. It was by one of my graduate students – an aggressive young man named Ralph MacMahon, who seemed temperamentally incapable of ever completing his own thesis – that she had been put onto an essay I had written on Collins and the origins of detective fiction, of which she was a fanatical reader. That was, I think, how it all started. Her mind instantly 'blown,' as she put it to me, she turned her now detonated attention to *Either/Either*; then to *The Vicious Spiral*; and the spell had been cast. She had become a Theorist.

Although she was already bound to Gillingwater, she came to my office one day to ask whether she might sit in on a few of my classes. I ought to have said no, these classes being oversubscribed as it was, and she assuredly was not about to plead; but in the end, intrigued in spite of myself, I agreed. I acceded too to Herb's not exactly unexpected request – when her thesis, in its clumsy, scattershot brilliance, began, about a half of the way in, to show incontrovertible symptoms of having succumbed to the creeping influence, the *'flu*, of the Theory, and he knew he was well out of his depth – to be his second opinion and in effect if not in name her director. She began fixing appointments to see me after class, ran into me by chance at a movie or in a coffee shop in town, occasionally with a hunched and sullen Ralph in tow, he not at all prone to dreamy idolatrous crushes, I could tell at once. One evening I even found myself seated just a couple of rows away from them at the Public Theater in Manhattan – but that, I fancy, was a *real* coincidence. (How her heart must have pounded at such an unscheduled windfall!) And when, finally, she had written that thesis of hers, and had somehow had it accepted for (vanity?) publication by some 'women's press' which hand-cranked its limp and sandpapery booklettes out of Carmel, N.J., she sent a copy to me with the ridiculous scribbled inscription: 'To L. S., this dedication to him for his dedication to me.'

Eight months had to elapse before I met her again. Out of the blue she made an appointment to come see me. I remember her entering my office as she had always done, her head a touch too erect for comfort, taking the same chair she had always taken, immediately crossing her legs and pulling her skirt down over the top of her right knee as expertly as if she were shooting a cuff. Wilfully or not, her severe and yet sexy features were offered up to me singly and separately like savory cocktail tidbits on a plate: her eyes, rendered oddly vulnerable by rimless granny glasses, the shape of Portuguese oysters; her hair, those enchantress's tresses of hers, which she would affectedly brush away from her eyes; her peachy cheeks that I would always subliminally associate with blowing into cupped palms in freezing weather; her own rather jittery hands peeping out, at the knuckles, from inside the straggling sleeves of a large loose sweater; her crossed legs surprisingly sheer and scissory.

She was tanned, she had been in Europe, and so we 'talked about Europe,' while I waited patiently for her to come to the point. And the point, when she did come to it, was that she planned to write – with or without authorization from me – my biography.

When she told me what it was she meant to do, my initial instinct was to look at my watch. This, merely a reflex on my part, an unfortunately timed one as I realized at once, she completely misunderstood. The smiling defiance tempered by apprehension with which she had announced her news to me swiftly drained from her features to be replaced by a moue of sulky disgruntlement. She was galled, nonplussed too, as I could see, that I had chosen no less than the crucial point in our interview, that at which she had played her trump card, to display what she presumably interpreted as my rude, fidgety impatience with her. Yet how could I convey to her that what I sought on my watch face was not the time but, as it were, time; that what I saw and all I saw (insofar as I saw anything at all) were the second and minute hands executing their immemorial hare-and-tortoise pursuit around the dial, the former advancing at a strictly measured pace, the latter, all wily invisible stealth, regularly outdistancing it from pit stop to pit stop? How was she to know that I had been waiting nearly seventeen years for someone to say to me what she had just said – for it, for this circumstance, to come about, as if it were finally its 'turn'? And how could I tell her that I had already made up my mind, possibly as late as at the very second she disclosed her project to me but already nevertheless, to forge ahead on my own? When things have to be said, they have to be said. Eventually they have to be said.

'Do I take it, Professor Sfax,' she asked in a tone suggesting that her previous temerity had once more got the upper hand, 'that your reservations –'

‘Oh but, you see, I have no reservations,’ I replied, smiling for the first time since my gaffe. ‘On the contrary, I approve – for all that *that’s* worth.’

Now she could barely credit how exorbitantly the situation seemed to have swung in her favor. ‘So you won’t, I mean to say, you won’t put any obstacles in my way?’

I assured her I would lend every assistance that could reasonably be expected of me – I believe in diplomacy and, if occasion permit, tolerance – and would even compose a short preliminary text to aid her in her research. But I felt bound to warn her in the same breath that there was little enough I *could* do, that in particular most of the data relating to an early period of my life could no longer be appreciated or verified, too much of the relevant documentation having been lost. It was far too soon in any event to worry about all that. Understandably, she had preferred to speak to me first before even approaching a publishing house, and I may as well admit, although I naturally forbore to say so to her, that at this premature stage of its development the entire enterprise struck me as having a very moot future indeed.

It was as I accompanied her to my office door that I cast my famously mild eyes over her fair, bony, very patrician, very ‘East Coast,’ and altogether pretty face, fringed as by the pasteboard curtain sashes of a toy theater by a tangle of reddish-brown hair.

'You realize,' I said, smiling still, 'that you will never *get* me? Nobody ever has.'

Now it was her turn to smile, toothily, almost girlishly – a smile as spontaneous and unpremeditated as a blush.

'Didn't you know I sculpted?' she suddenly asked, as if it somehow 'showed,' for how I was otherwise supposed to know such a thing I couldn't imagine.

'No – really?'

'Only figurative stuff, I'm afraid. Heads, mostly. But they do say I'm very strong on likenesses. I mean to capture yours – if you'll let me.'

I made the primly strategic reply that first it would be for a publisher to let her – 'Where there's a will there's a way,' I murmured, '– or rather, where there's a way there's a will.'

She laughed; then, with a handshake, we said goodbye.

I returned to my desk to think over this strange little scene. I looked again at my watch, but this time just to see the time. Her appointment had been at five and it was by a minute gone half-past. So – it had taken only half-an-hour to cast the die. And it was a sculptress who cast it. A sculptress? Is everyone fated to have at least one sculptress in their life? Astrid! Her very name was a signifier of the 'creative' in all its poignant horror. No, truly no, I couldn't entrust my head to her.

I checked that I had no more appointments that afternoon and, satisfied that the rest of the day was mine to do with as I pleased, I switched on my Apple Mac computer. I opened a new file, to which I gave the password *Hermes*, and for a good five or six minutes sat there staring at the screen, the blank white screen-page, until at last I set to typing (I'm a two-finger man, basically – or even one, the left forefinger serving as not much more than the right's assistant, intervening, like the less agile half of a tennis doubles partnership, to bag an occasional comma or apostrophe) the forty-five pages that you have just been reading.

Reader, I tell a lie. English, indeed, has always been for me *a language to lie in*, the language in which I have sought to dissolve or destroy the past – the past which not even God, as they say, can alter. Yet in my identity as liar, as equally in that identity in relation to which I have lied, I am, you must understand, the fatally preordained product of generation upon generation of my fathers and hence the repository of their errors, their violence, their crimes; from such an explosive powder train no one, not I, not you, not anyone, has ever contrived to escape. We are perhaps tempted, perhaps even attempt, to accord ourselves an entirely new past, one of which we might have preferred to be the product instead of that of which we are in truth. It is, however, a perilous strategy, because it will never be possible to trace the boundaries of any denial of the past, and because the newly invented nature is likely to be weaker after all than that which preceded it, the creator being always, of necessity, stronger than the created.

It was aboard the Italian ship removing me from Europe that I fell in with Tito. This ship, the reverse of the luxuriously appointed ocean greyhound, the floating America, that I, ingenuous traveler as I was, dreamt that it might be, was a grimy and ancient steamer out of Palermo which, when I boarded it at Marseilles, already creaked and heaved under the weight of its pathetically huddled masses, as well as of the mattresses, cribs, chairs, lamps, cardboard suitcases, and birdcages without which it seems no contemporary exodus is ever quite complete. I shared an airless cabin, of barely notional comfort, inches above the waterline, with three Italians in their early thirties whose stevedores' chests, as tight and tough as breastplates, strained at their undershirts. These white undershirts, which went unchanged throughout the entire voyage, could almost be read as calendars, a gangrenous patch of sweat seeping upward from below the belt's Equator to chart the number of days we had been afloat.

None of them spoke French, and only Ernesto, or Tito, as he at once invited me to call him, any English, albeit very fallibly. Well enough, though, for me to understand – for he had a wearing confessional streak, especially when his comrades were snoring their heads off in their bunks – that they weren't stevedores at all or anything resembling it, but former Fascist militiamen from the Romagna region who had fled together to Sicily after Mussolini's fall and been sheltered by the Mafia to which they had had to shell out in protection money most of the small fortune they had amassed. With a monstrous imperturbability he let me finger his passport, false, naturally, and told me that in exchange for the last of their hard-earned loot an American army officer had arranged for them to emigrate.

Tito was a slightly inexplicable individual, a somewhat richer personality than I had any right to expect under the circumstances, thin-skinned and easily offended, but also a moral illiterate. When he recounted the minor atrocities he had committed, mostly having to do with castor oil, and none, of those at least he sottishly confessed to, involving anyone's death, he would plead pure, non-ideological opportunism. The least of all evils, opportunism was to be his defense, his alibi, forever thereafter. He had been no Fascist, he would say, he hated the

Fascists, he would spit just at the sound of the word – but, but, a man has to make his way up in the world (this coaxed out of him in a canny Italianate wheedle) and in a Fascist world that way will be Fascist too. And the opportunist would bare his perfect teeth in a movie star's grin.

We spent a good deal of complicitous time together, he and I. Sitting either cross-legged in the middle or sidesaddle at the edge of my lower bunk, our heads bowed, almost grazing, beneath its low, usually distended canvas ceiling, we beguiled the daily, hourly monotony of the voyage playing chess together.

Tito was the incomparably superior tactician, never at a loss for a meaningful move and greeting every meaningless move I made, every flailing and uncorroborated stratagem, by shaking his head, sometimes even scratching it, like a country bumpkin in a slapstick farce, pointing his knobby, calloused forefinger with its long, hard, almondy, and lethal fingernail at the offending piece, and in his gentle baffled voice inquiring, comically, 'Because?' – for he had not gotten the hang of the difference between 'why' and 'because,' both of them, in his native tongue, 'perché.' And when I would occasionally all but shove my reluctant King into check, Tito audibly exhaled his despair of me, rolling his eyes heavenward, their whites matching the whites of his teeth, and groaning, 'Because, Léo? Because you did that?'

Because? Because I did that? That phrase, that gloriously grotesque solecism of his, I heard again and again at night, at four or five o'clock in the morning, foreshortening my past while the ship would plow on into my future. Because? Because?

It was one evening in 1941, in my parents' salon, at a dinner for Arno Breker, Hitler's pet sculptor, that with tortuous aplomb Alain Laubreaux invited me to contribute to *Je suis partout* a weekly column reporting on current literary and cultural events. I could certainly have declined without incurring the faintest risk to myself, and I hesitated – and in fact I continued to hesitate long after that original encounter of ours – before informing him of my decision. Within the hesitation, though, there was already contained the affirmative. I had taken the decision, there in the drawing room, I had maneuvered myself toward it quite as far as I could without actually coming out and saying yes, it was little more than *amour-propre* which made me hold off for the moment, a promising young comer's desire not to be seen too hungrily leaping upon the first offer to fall into his lap.

Laubreaux had never been a regular guest in my father's house, and I rather suppose he had invited himself that evening. He was the very type of collaborator who sees his main chance in getting in on the ground floor of a calamity, the born loser who multiplies his failure and his country's together and from these two negatives produces at least a personal positive. It wasn't the war which made him a scoundrel (in the thirties he had published under his own name a novel written by some young inmate of the Santé who had then seen it confiscated from him by a warder, none other than Laubreaux's father), but it was the war which gave him a dunghill on top of which he could crow and allowed his morbidities a free run at last. As the theater critic of *Je suis partout*, and something of a cultural eminence among the collaborationist press, he was a man of whom it was said that no one would dare to be his enemy or care to be his friend.

He approached me after dinner with his proposition, tapping his shoecap nervously with his cane as he might have drummed his fingers on a tabletop, and he couched it in an image that didn't quite come off – something to do with 'bottling the essence' of Paris 'just as *notre chère* Mademoiselle Chanel has done.'

I was astonished, I dare say also obscurely flattered, although at first I obeyed a natural instinct to refuse, pleading my lack of competence and experience.

There was a lengthy silence. I ran a clockwise finger along the slim rim of my champagne glass and waited for him to speak again.

'You *would* be free, you know,' he said at last.

'Free?'

'Oh – to write as you wish. To say what you please. I never interfere. Besides, I know – we all know – that you're the sort who can be trusted.'

'Trusted?' Once more I found myself artlessly echoing the last word he had said, as in some childish singsong game. Whereupon Laubreaux glanced beyond me, over my shoulder, which prompted me to take a look there with him; then just as abruptly he turned to face me again and, strangely, pressed his cane's metal tip hard upon the toe of my shoe, as if he were hoping thus to nail me to the spot.

'To do justice to this – this scum: to these politicians whose names have all been filed away in the Quai des Orfèvres under bribery, graft, misappropriation of public funds; these busy press barons who nevertheless always find the time to handpick their new little office boys; these so-called financiers never more than one deal ahead of the fraud squad; these self-styled aristocrats who've been blackballed from the Jockey Club for surreptitiously adding a tiny bit extra to their stakes after the winning number has come up; these actors whose best performances are destined for a select few in the *pissotières* along the boulevard Sébastopol; these *grandes dames* of literature who'd show their unwiped bottoms in the music-hall if it helped to pump up circulation. To do justice to *that*.'

I was all the more stupefied by this discharge of bile in the drawing room of a man, my father, whose guest, gatecrasher or not, he after all was, in that in his denunciatory passion he had much overdrawn the glitter and ado of the company, even as he vilified it, and I couldn't help suspecting that the tirade had been delivered something short of extempore, that it was his set speech on 'the decadence of French society.' And since, as I could well note, Laubreaux relished my stupefaction nearly as much as he relished his own self-appointed role of professional fiend, I was utterly unprepared for the paroxysmal changing of gears represented by what he had to say next.

'Listen to me, young man. I know what you must think of me, tut-tut, yes I do – but it's of little consequence. What you've got to understand, you and all your generation, is that you no longer have the luxury of *deciding* what it is you're *going* to do.' (Each italicized word represents the tiny vicious aggravation of pressure that he would apply from his cane onto my shoe.) 'Everything there ever will be in France, or in Europe, is already in place. So what it is you plan to do with your life you must start to do at once – the future, you see, will simply be *too late*.' (Here he gave one tap on the toe of my shoe for *too*, another, distinctly separate one for *late*.) 'Now you're a clever young man – I know you are and you know you are – and the sole success worth its powder is success in the line of a natural gift. So don't resist it. Whatever you do, don't exile yourself from the future, from the only future you have. Go with your gifts. A clever man can argue anything if he sets his mind to it, and, I repeat, there are *no other options*.'

I won't pretend that among all these apothegms there was not a good deal of driveling connective tissue but that was the nub of it, and what struck me at the time was how abstract it sounded, how almost metaphysical, especially by contrast with what had preceded it, as if I were being tendered an unrejectable blessing of tremendous spiritual regeneration and not just the chance to chart a space for myself, much sooner than I should ever have dared to hope – for I was still in my early twenties – in a world at whose hem I had until then only, if gratefully, pawed.

I let his proposal ride for a week before I definitively took him up on it, as also on the suggestion that I write the column under a *nom de guerre*, a fairly common practice even before the war made of it less of a caprice than, often, an imperative. It was, I should say, nothing more than a hedging of bets on my own part, a mask to be shed when circumstances permitted it, when the wind in short would have started to blow in one irreversible direction; and I hit upon for myself, I thought, a wonderfully appropriate pseudonym: Hermes. Hermes, who made the first lyre from out of a tortoise's shell and invented the Pan pipes, Hermes the divine messenger, the god of commerce and flight, the thief who was never caught red-handed.

I returned to print. During the next three years, until the late months of 1943, Hermes published upward of a hundred and fifty articles, articles widely acknowledged as being of an exceptionally 'virile,' 'patriotic,' 'exalting' stamp, moderated, when necessary, by an almost feminine finesse. And if the name I was making was not yet my own, the secret of my alias was of a type that is virtually impossible to keep for any length of time and I was gradually able, in those heady early days of the virtual certainty of final and durable German victory, to bask in my own wretched glory.

I did, though, vaguely disappoint Laubreaux with the first few of my articles. Feeling gingerly about plunging right in, and determined to be quite as devious as my masters as to how far at this stage of the war I ought to commit myself, I began my stint on a coolly frivolous note, my status for a month or two rarely, and even then barely, rising above that of the gossip columnist. I would cover the dress rehearsal of some new boulevard comedy by Guitry or an abjectly 'Wagnerian' ballet by Lifar or the private view of the latest Van Dongen show. Yet I was not at all backward, in however trivial the context, in putting to the test Laubreaux's promise not to interfere. I would twit the preposterous 'sensitivity' displayed by the mutton-headed Parisian *élégantes* who had started to fashion new hats out of old newspapers, as to precisely the tenor of those headlines that risked being most readable to passers-by; as also that of some radio announcer from Longchamp hastening to dispel the ambiguity that might otherwise have surrounded one of the winners, Isaac, by reassuring his listeners that it was the horse's name, not the jockey's.

Such affable audacities passed, as the French put it, like a letter through the post and, still cautiously testing the temperature as I went gropingly on, I was at last emboldened by my liberty to turn myself to the great issues, the huge and only real issues, of the time. I would perch atop my column like Simon Stylites atop his, despairing publicly, over the years, in article after article, of 'the future possibilities of French culture,' of that culture's endemic, seemingly ineradicable chauvinism when confronted with the 'near-mystical' era which Europe in its entirety had already entered, an era of, as I gaudily predicted, 'suffering, intoxication, and redemption.' I chided a number of prominent collaborationist writers, Montherlant, Chardonne, Drieu la Rochelle, Paul Morand, for what I felt was the inadequacy of their sympathetic yet still overly anguished and subjectivist response to the spiritual foundations on which the new European unity was even then being erected and I argued that there could be no inherent reason to grant a man of letters such authority in a realm of human behavior that manifestly escaped his competence. I declared from the flimsy pedestal of my own usurped authority that these war years, however long they might last, and however 'tragic' their day-to-day realities, might be most fruitfully viewed as a meditative pause for the occupied nations before the revolutionary tasks that would have to be undertaken at their end; and that the primary imperative for all good Europeans was the realization that no distinction could any longer be made, as some feet-dragging 'intellectuals' were clearly struggling to make, between Germany and Hitlerism. On the contrary, I wrote, in a piece that was particularly admired, 'the war will only have united the more intimately those two quite kindred realities that the Hitlerian soul and the German soul have been since the beginning, fusing them into a single unique force.' This, I insisted, was a significant phenomenon, for it meant that the future of Europe would now have to be anticipated exclusively 'within the framework of the German genius' – hence that collaboration with the occupier was an 'imperative obvious to any objective observer.'

Each of us falls from his own height, and each height, of whatever mean measure of elevation, can nevertheless yet be fallen from. These articles of mine, judged so extravagantly at the time, were common, putrid Nazi hack work, sterile, bogus, repetitious, humiliating for me, here and now, to recall. And since the merely bogus in literature, in any form and at any level of literature, must fatally descend into the obscene and the pornographic, somewhere between the frivolity of my journalistic juvenalia to a terrifying day in 1943, when a photograph of me appeared alongside sixty-odd others in the 'Traitors' Gallery' of a quite widely circulated Resistance pamphlet, an inexplicable and yet also unforgivable thing seems to have happened to me. By an itinerary that continues to escape me I had somehow shifted in my allegiance from the passive collaborationism of the *attentistes*, as they were called, those who deigned to cooperate with the occupier only and reluctantly in order to secure for themselves and their country a tolerable life in the irresistible 'New Order,' to the luxuriant and ecstatic treason practised by those who would unreservedly assume the values of the thousand-year Reich. I had grown, in short, less concerned with the best interests of France than with the best interests of Germany.

It isn't easy for me now, how many years on, to follow the trace of so surreptitiously gradual a transference, to date with any real exactness my first delirious immersions in the Nazis' peculiar logic and lexicon. But already in the spring of 1941, in an article on the role of the fine arts in a time of war, I wrote that 'a sincere artist cannot, can never, renounce his proper regional character, destined as it has been by blood and soil.' Blood and soil? How could I, so consummately my own man, as I believed, even in the worse than suspect context of *Je suis partout*, have let slip such a damning formulation into my discourse? *Blood and soil.* That I, I of all people, allowed myself to be snared into spouting such metaphysical flummery!

Nor is that all. When things have to be said, eventually they have to be said. In the first days of February 1942, when the outcome of the war was in the balance, when rumors of the incredible, related to certain matters of literal life and death, and worse than death, had became so many and so confused that I no longer know the true extent of what I might or might not have known then, I published a long piece on 'the Jewish question,' and specifically on the Judaization – another coinage from Dr Goebbels' piggy-bank – of European literature.

Oh, for that unsubtle time I could be subtlety itself! Resolved to retain the aloofness of trenchancy and tone which had become Hermes' trademark, his recognized contribution to any debate, I took pains never to use the term 'anti-Semitism' without first qualifying it as 'vulgar' or 'primitive.' Thus, depending on whether the reader's eye read the conjunction of noun and adjective concavely or convexly, so to speak, such a fastidious disinclination to leave the word alone could mean either that I held anti-Semitism to be vulgar and primitive in its very essence or else that I was holding out for some 'higher' anti-Semitism, one that would be not vulgar but refined, not primitive but modern. Nor was I myself so vulgar and primitive as to attack Jewish writers for having appropriated our culture just as Jewish bankers (so the weary old argument ran) had appropriated our capital. I proposed rather that their part in the evolution of this culture had been minimal, trashy, and totally undeserving of the passions it had inflamed, that the Jewish influence had been but a minor 'pollutant,' that – but here I'm no longer able to paraphrase, I can but quote – that 'a solution to the problem that would lead to the creation of a Jewish colony isolated from Europe would not have, for the cultural life of the West, regrettable consequences. It would lose, in all, some personalities of mediocre worth and would continue, as in the past, to develop according to its higher laws of evolution.'

Reader, I wrote that. I who write these words wrote those atrocious words, committed that atrocity. Because? Because I did it?

I can vouch for at least one fact. I am not, nor was I then, nor ever, an anti-Semite. It would be as inconceivable for me to let myself be corrupted by the metaphysics of race as by any other grand, mindless metaphysical category, to begin with God. But never forget, I say, never forget the environment of my formative years. My grandfather, the pale Parnassian poet, the anti-cosmopolitan. My father, among the habitués of whose house were Jewish artists but of whom I also knew, insofar as I knew anything without the transparent testimony of my eyes, that the canvases he sold to Otto Abetz and his cronies had been purchased, at a shyster's take-it-or-leave-it price, from Jewish acquaintances desperate to liquidate what assets they still possessed and leave the country. My parents' Gentile friends, who, no haters of the Jews whom they must have encountered, most of them, on a nearly daily basis, were all the same prone to speaking of them in the raffishly impudent style considered to be quite the thing in the years I refer to. The very noun 'Jew,' now practically a gaffe in any respectable company, was still enunciable in those days without one's having to adjectivize its angles into 'Jewish'; a woman could still be described without insult as a 'Jewess.'

If I cite these examples, it isn't to exculpate my own life's Nazi interlude or mitigate my disastrous initiative – I will never be able to do that – but only to make the point that the route I had to travel out of such reprehensible irrationalities started further back, far further back, than anyone is in a position to judge today. And it strikes me now that those prewar articles of mine in *Le Libre Arbitre*, however unimpeachable the stance they took against the looming aggressor, were already pollinated with the seed of what I would subsequently let so venenously flower in *Je suis partout*. There was something more than slightly dubious, was there not, in their insistent reiteration of such terms as 'barbarians' and 'order' and the 'decadence' of 'Occidental civilization.' There could be no doubt, I repeat, about my opposition to the Nazi movement. Nevertheless, detectable in my discourse, there remained the lambent traces, the still flickering embers, of an occult and certainly unconscious attachment to the very codes and practices of the ideology I claimed to oppose. (That the analysis of this process would become my life's work is an irony even I have learned to savor.) If right and left could share a word like 'order,' and each find in it its respective truth, it could only be that some real ambiguity lay deep and ineradicable at its core, and that no leftist use of it would ever be able to rid itself of its rightist, indeed antidemocratic and totalitarian, instincts. Then, too, the pernicious paradox of the word 'Occidental' is that its sole and instant effect on the European reader is to remind him of its opposite, of the Orient, of that desert of sallow-skinned Otherness of which the tow-headed honey-golden Aryan blondness beloved of the Nazi imagination was precisely the etherealized countertype. To denounce Nazism, in short, I had unwittingly been using the Nazis' own language and rhetoric.

There, for the Theory's unbelievers, is a classic instance of how a text, alas, may write its author.

Yet it was, after all, an initiative on my part to write for *Je suis partout*, and write what I did. I chose to do so, where I might not have done; and having made that first calamitous move on the chessboard I might still with impunity have drawn a line at its basest implications. Was it, then, mere vulgar opportunism, no more elevated than that of which Tito was to be so bland an apologist, that I let myself sink to a depth of abjection that Laubreaux had never asked or expected of me?

In my defense I would say only this: I was a gifted young man of twenty-two who had a desperate longing to write, who feverishly sought an outlet for his gifts, and who believed that he would be condemning himself, in resisting the temptation to collaborate, to an ineluctable life sentence, a régime of mute mediocrity, under the New Order. It will not be easy for some, I know, simply not possible for others, to appreciate how I could be driven to such lengths by the passion to write, by the terror that clamped itself upon me at the thought of waiting for years, conceivably for ever, to say everything that I had to say, and to say it publicly. However intensely at the same time I might have desired to be one with the crowd, to cast off my burden of genius – the only word that will do at the age of twenty-two – I knew that I was damned by that genius, as damned as any Catholic in a world of atheists who longs equally to disburden himself of a fatal cross of faith and guilt, who cries out to his God, 'Why me? Why have I been oppressed with this unsought and unwanted revelation? Why can't I partake of the simple, harmless, godless pleasures of life like those around me?' – and who, like the artist with a heaven in his head, will ever be thrown back into lonely intimacy with his fate.

There was the sadistic nicety of my agony: to have been singled out from the crowd by my brilliance of intellect and, just when that intellect attains its majority, to have it denied its natural forum. Who, then, would blame me for accepting the single forum that *was* offered me, not one I would have chosen had everything else been equal but one I naively imagined I could turn to my own – and they weren't to start with so very selfish – ends? That I concluded my term at *Je suis partout* peddling the same wretched commonplaces as the stooges and lackeys and bootlickers with whom I had to share the newspaper's pages but from whom within its offices I scrupulously kept my distance no less than my counsel is to my everlasting shame. But that fact, too, beyond one man's personal shortcomings, contains a moral of sorts, a moral concerning the power of a medium to overwhelm any single message that may be emitted within it.

I was not a member of the Resistance, ever, even if I did ask Paul, in the circumstances I have described, to speak on my behalf. Without exactly refusing me at once, he held out little comfort; so wholly unpersuadable did he himself, a friend, seem to be of my potential usefulness to the organization, I had scant cause to hope that his superiors, who didn't know me at all, would take my application any more seriously. Nor apparently did they, for a week or so later Paul told me that it was out of the question.

I had been perfectly in earnest, although God knows how I would ever have reconciled the two halves of my existence if I had been accepted: this was in 1942 and I had already signed Hermes' name to a score of articles. I confess it titillated me that Paul suspected no ulterior or underhand motive behind my comings and goings or that my life might have been just as furtive and duplicitous in its way as his own. It was at the newspaper's offices, while I was understood by my friends to be on the other side of town, studying in one of the libraries near the boulevard Saint-Michel, that I would compose my articles; and what the three of us lived off – grandfather's legacy, as I had them believe – was in reality the ill-gotten salary that I earned from them. Or it was, I should say, a part of that salary. By only the first of the paradoxes that were to pursue me thereafter, I didn't dare allow any of us to live or eat as well as we could have, even for those stark and strict and frugal years, lest suspicion be aroused by an uncommonly generous inflow of funds. Like so many others, we half starved; and the surplus I carefully secreted in my bedroom at the house in the Chevreuse valley.

This state of affairs lasted until the day, nearly a year later, when Paul failed to return to the apartment. He had not, according to what a distraught Louise could tell me afterwards, been on any particular 'job,' any clandestine assignment, but was picked up by the Gestapo while whiling away a half-hour with a couple of companions on the terrace of a café on one of the *grands boulevards*. I was immediately seduced by the idea that through my 'influence,' slight as this undoubtedly was, it might yet be possible to 'do something' for him, which would also become a way whereby, assuming my wire-pulling obtained Paul's release before it was too late, I could present to my now indebted and forgiving friends my conduct until then as a benign *fait accompli*, a very blessing in disguise. I soon came to my senses, however, realized the width and depth of the abyss that separated me from the true inner concentrations of power, and made no overtures to my employers at *Je suis partout*. Quite the reverse, in fact. The thought of what had happened to Paul, which affected me less than it did Louise but did affect me greatly nevertheless, the thought above all of what I could guess *was* happening to him at that very hour in a cellar in the rue Lauriston, cured me for ever of the folly of continuing to support a cause whose ultimate victory in any case, in the latter half of 1943, no longer looked quite the foregone conclusion that it had. Without either an apology or an explanation, I put Hermes down, as they say of lame animals, and ceased all collaboration with Laubreaux and his egregious rag.

Louise and I went on living together in the old apartment, sharing at first only our grief, then, after what we could no longer put off thinking of as Paul's death, slowly drawing closer to one another. We ourselves had been barely disturbed by the Gestapo in the wake of his arrest – a single visit made sinisterly late at night but actually entailing nothing more than an on-the-spot examination of our papers – and the sole subsequent risk posed to the smooth course of our relationship was the distribution of the pamphlet that bore my snapshot. A copy of the thing, which I instantly burned, was anonymously forwarded to me, I presume by Laubreaux. But Louise had only ever had a superficial contact with her lover's comrades, and the fact that I, even if living quite openly with her on the Ile Saint-Louis, was untroubled by the Resistance at that time tended to confirm what I'd always suspected and what I now had very good reason to be grateful for: that Paul never did 'speak for me,' he never did mention my name as of someone potentially useful to the cell.

When the Liberation came, the position I found myself in was a naturally unpleasant one; yet the difficulties I experienced, although more than I hoped, were after all rather less than I feared. In a period that saw Guitry imprisoned and Brasillach executed, the low order of significance ascribed to my own offense – like that, indeed, of my father – was demonstrated by the fact that, privately reviled by the panel of questioners before which I had been summoned to appear, I wasn't in the end publicly denounced, not so publicly, anyway, for it to reach Louise's ears.

Until my departure for the States she and I lived hardly less modestly than during the war itself. I started to read as many English-language books as I could find, as many too of a type that resembled the work I might one day choose to write myself – were I ever to write again. Virtually our only luxuries were excursions to the American movies, by then often four or five years old, which arrived in Paris after the war in a rash and a rush, like some joyous return of the repressed. Louise earned a little something as a *scripte*, a continuity girl, for Pathé and I not much more as a translator from English, of technical and even military documents, but also, once, of a novel by Somerset Maugham. Yet, hard as these times were, it didn't once occur to me that I could always start lifting from the money that was cached away in my parents' house. *That* was destined for our emigration, a subject I didn't care to broach with Louise until I was absolutely sure there were real grounds for hoping it was going to happen.

For the cargo of my indiscretions lay heavy and inert within me – for me the war wasn't over. These years were terrible ones for the French, these horrific nearly year-long winters of whose mythic rawness and rigor Barthes has somewhere written; and yet amid the rubble of our battered continent the living stirred. Everything appeared possible, thinkable, once more, as at the outset of some great adventure; even as, in a macabre prelude to the 'big picture,' the first all too credibly incredible newsreel images of the liberation of the camps were vouchsafed us, were vouchsafed me, me, defenseless and silent in a movie theater illuminated only by the monochrome radiance of dead Jews, these images seemed, the more horrible they were, to belong to an already dim, no longer intelligible history on which we had only to turn our backs to face our future.

Our future, not mine: I was banished, I knew, from the dense and vibrant collective. Not Paris alone, not France, but Europe altogether was the scene of a crime to which in my mean and ignoble fashion I had been a party. If I were to have remained, I might have seen myself becoming what? – the wandering Nazi? This was outrageous. I was still young, I wanted to live. Europe was bearing down upon me like the sort of Gothick torture chamber on whose victim the ceiling descends and the walls contract, and I came to feel with ever more conviction that my reformation could lie only in America, in its bright patchwork of opportunity, its whole candid candied hugeness, although I had little inkling then of what I might be capable of doing there and whether I might prosper at it, and still less hope that it would offer me the intellectual and spiritual salvation that it has.

It was just a few months short of the date of our departure, when I was already up to my elbows in forms and applications, that I returned from a long weekend in the country to discover that Louise had gone and left me this note:

> 'Léo, I'm leaving you. The apartment is yours for as long as you continue paying its rent. I've taken my things and Paul's. The rest – including things I don't remember who they belong to – you can have. Don't ever try to find me. I know who you are. I should say I know who you were, but I find it awfully hard to accept

you aren't still that person. I've given this thing a lot of thought and I can't genuinely find it in me – or in you – to believe that you were in any way directly responsible for what happened to Paul. But I don't know and I'll never know even if you told me and I couldn't live with you without knowing. ~~I would have~~ That's all.'

It was left unsigned almost as if she had wanted to lend it the quality of an anonymous denunciation.

Actually, the question of finding her hardly arose. Louise's family was of relatively modest means, more so since the end of the war, and even wishing as she did not to confront me in person it was unlikely she would ever quit her job at Pathé. A straightforward inquiry at the film company's office would have been enough to bring us face to face. It was my feeling, however, on rereading her note, that our situation was perhaps best left as it was. My own position until then – until someone, as was clear, had informed on me – had not been all that different from the position in which she found herself now. Could I after all have lived happily with her, and possibly married her, without wondering whether and what she knew about me? There had been no public sequel to my disgrace, it's true, but a history of the terrible years would eventually have to be written – although probably in years rather than in months to come – and the pettiness of my part in it certainly offered no guarantee that to the last I would be spared from exposure.

So I left without her, and though she was to surface briefly in the American half of my existence I never saw her again.

Strangely enough, Tito, whom I wished good luck to, along with his two thuggish traveling companions, as we were about to disembark at Ellis Island, would also reemerge in my life if with no special consequence to it. In New York in the early seventies, not many months after my appointment to New Harbor, the show trial was held of a trio of middle-level Mafia racketeers. There, on the *New York Times*'s front page, a lot svelter and sleeker, with a garish chinchilla ripple streaking his glossy black hair like the marking of some exotic animal, yet unmistakably the foxy charmer I'd known, was a photograph of a handcuffed, glumly defiant Tito – Ernesto Cavazzone – being squeezed out through the cramped corridor of a courthouse past a mob of reporters. I followed his trial with genuine interest and was perversely tempted to attend it. That, I finally didn't do – but I did note with some amusement, from the extracts that were published of his cross-examination, that his years in America had educated him in at least one thing: the difference between 'why' and 'because.' It wasn't enough to save him, though. He was found as guilty as he all too manifestly was and received a ninety-nine-year prison sentence. Poor Tito.

A biography and a life belong to two quite dissimilar categories. Raphaël and his wife, the Greenwich Village bookstore, our Sunday afternoon readings, my bare little walk-up on Eighth Street – all of these were exactly as I have described them. But they were subterraneously linked by something else that I did not describe – my neurotic concern and compulsion to *keep my head down*.

I was at first perfectly content with my obscurity, I didn't despise my set of friends or secretly mock their pretensions to culture and intellect. All too quickly, however, I began to be haunted by the presentiment of a potential for some kind of distinction, of uniqueness, perhaps even of greatness, having forever to be left dormant, in eternal abeyance, within me. It was the fear of that untapped virtuality, the craving, even in surroundings as mediocre as mine were at the time, to express to some negligible degree all that I was bursting to express, that obliged me to take such ludicrous pains with my Mallarmé paper, whose reception, I may say, caused my youthful pulses to throb. And when it had been taken for publication the effect it had upon me was exactly that of a single drink on a reformed alcoholic: along with the natural exhilaration it brought me came an exacerbation of my self-loathing and a dread, absurdly premature at this stage of my ascension, of the perils of such publicity, the peril, if it were to continue and expand, of an eventual disclosure of my past. It was merely the first rung of the ladder, I realized, but I can only say that I knew, even then I *knew*, that brilliance such as mine, if allowed to shine at all, must ultimately train a floodlight on the entire course of my life and every maggoty recess of its history. I knew that – yet how could I resist? Could anyone have resisted? I wanted to live, not merely to breathe. I wanted a second chance, a good chance that would be commensurate with the evil chance that Laubreaux had extended me. How could I hold back, how could I reject what was being offered me in so Americanly liberal a fashion – the chance no longer to toil in some obscure store, handling other men's books the way a bank teller must handle other men's money, the chance to teach courses and write articles on these books, the chance, at long last, to write and publish books of my own? Who would blame me for not resisting?

Yet, on each rung of the ladder, at each of my professional and social promotions, I paused, I trembled, drew back, telling myself that the course I was on was a fatal one that must lead sooner or later to my perdition. As I advanced toward my apotheosis so also was I advancing towards my extinction, my utter destruction. The terrible irony of it all was that, with the passing of time, the danger to me of my growing reputation, instead of receding, only increased; the higher I rose, the more blind, because the ever more warranted, became my fears. I would feel at first compelled to refuse everything that the world laid before me, refuse again and again – until, inevitably, a resurgent will to live, to express what I had to express, would prevail, and I would accept. Whence no doubt derived my reputation, among those whose desire it was to help me, for a heroic modesty, a refreshing rare resistance to putting myself forward, to rushing along my advancement.

For the same reason I was afraid of ever marrying, lest my wife would take the normal spousal interest in her husband's family, wish to meet them, and learn perhaps from my doting, talkative, indiscriminate mother of, if probably not my own disgrace, then my father's; and I had to content myself with a series of casual and not often happy affairs to which my temperament ill-suited me. I thought too, by another sorry irony, of adopting a *nom de guerre* for my writings in English, as if the pieces I had published under the pseudonym of Hermes now seemed to me so shameful I felt I had to conceal *that name* under a new pseudonym. But the notion occurred to me a good little while after I'd already started to make something of a place for myself in America; beyond which, it struck me disagreeably, at a time when my ambition was above all to expiate the perfidies of my European life, as a betrayal of my citizenship.

Even Stradivarius must have heard sounds inside his head more ravishing than any produced on one of his violins; but he had to make the violins to hear the sounds. I could not live and go on living with all the sounds I had ever heard, all the thoughts I had ever had, immured inside my head. The articles I wrote, more and more numerous as these were to become over the years, finally ceased altogether to satisfy my real intellectual needs, and my frustration was all the greater in that I felt forced to reject an initial offer from New Harbor's own publishing house, when I was already assuming the status of a crumpled and messianic guru on the campus, to have them collected in a single volume. For all my ludicrous paranoid precautions theretofore, *that*, I knew, would assuredly start the process of sealing my fate, simply on the question of supplying the publishing house with the author's statutory little biography, his potted 'bio,' to accompany his photograph on the book's inside flap. I gave as the reason for declining the honor my feeling that few of these occasional pieces of mine seemed to me truly to merit the canonization of hard covers, an attitude of self-abnegation so positively unheard-of in the ferociously competitive academic groves that it could only reinforce the general perception of me yet again as a near-saintly figure, a living reproach to a profession full of phonies, that sweet, gentle, modest man – ruthless, though, in debate – who by the sheer force of his intellect had succeeded in rising from penurious obscurity to a position of the very highest eminence – an inspiration in short, quaint proof that not even intellectuals were excluded from the American Dream.

My appearance helped. There are few, perhaps unexpectedly few, photographs of me in existence and it would be impossible for me to tap out on this computer some solemn description of my physical distinguishing marks, as passports put it. But I had once been told, by Gillingwater, as I recall, that I bore a very pronounced facial likeness to the actor Clifton Webb, less the pinched-nose prissiness that was his trademark; he, Gillingwater, added that the rimless bifocals that I wore more frequently in my jacket's breast pocket than on my nose were a pretty poor exchange for the ribboned pince-nez that my eyes and, according to him, general old-world posture were crying out for. I mention such trivia simply to communicate the effect I was making on New Harbor at that time, of a modest, honest, unmarried, unhurried, baggily humane and aloof thinker, the one honorable man, to paraphrase Raymond Chandler, who walked down the mean streets of the prettiest campus in the United States.

*

With the publication of *Either/Either* I became the bemused object of whole new levels and layers of idolatry. It may seem illogical that, having rejected the New Harbor Press's idea of a volume of my collected journalism, I would subsequently offer it unasked and uncommissioned an entirely original work. My motives were complicated. At Breen, at Amherst, and Cornell I had restrained myself, held myself in, done more than competently what had been required of me but done only that nevertheless, allowed my brilliance an airing only very occasionally in articles here and there, and all in the hope that I might taste something of the success I would otherwise have more fully known without risking the personal calamity that the wake of that fuller success would certainly have brought me sooner or later. But what had happened? Was I ignored? Was I allowed to work away quietly in my own chosen little corner? Not at all. The more neglectful I obliged myself to be where the furtherance of my career was concerned, the more immediately and, it sometimes seemed, automatically was I rewarded with preferment, as if I had only to be reticent about a new post to be begged to accept it: conspicuously, and after all sincerely, putting myself out of the running for a job would in short turn out to be the quickest way of securing it. If, as I say, my perennial fear had been that the better-known I became, the better the likelihood of my exposure, by the time I joined the faculty at New Harbor I was beginning to think I could hardly lose more by risking more.

There was the additional fact that I was fifty-four when the book was published and that I'd lived nearly as long in America as in France. The events the thought of whose revelation so paralyzed me had taken place at least a decade before most of my students were born and it struck me that they were much less easily conjurable now than had once been the case. My age, too, was beginning to weigh heavily upon me: like a career woman who feels within her the uneasy stirrings of a too long languishing maternal instinct, I realized that, if I were ever to publish seriously at all, this would be virtually my last stab at it.

I was mindful all the same, as a final precaution, not to let the ideas I put forward in the book stray too far from theories that were already in vogue in Paris – so that, my reasoning ran, there would be little incentive to have it translated 'back' into French. Thus I was startled by the degree to which it seemed my own peculiar cast of mind had nevertheless contrived to make itself felt in a text that for any truly informed reader contained nothing very novel – just as that cast of mind had been making itself felt throughout the years of my self-imposed purgatory. My own opinion was that *Either/Either* was the work of some mere second-hand visionary of déjà vu. Yet to my amazement and horror, and no doubt because it had been written and published in English without the palliative refinement of having first to be translated, my contemporaries received the book as if it were a revelation.

Whatever the cause, it had the success that it had, and all my old terrors were abruptly revived. I had become the thing that I had always struggled against becoming: a celebrity. My students worshiped me, and my colleagues now addressed me with a new shading of favor and consideration in their voices which intimated that something in New Harbor's eternal power plays had crucially shifted to my advantage. I would begin to get invited more and more frequently to international conferences – at which, however, as I realized, it would not have been so unlikely, not in the least a coincidence, for me to encounter some young and fashionable Parisian linguist for whom my name rang a feeble, distant bell; or, worse still, someone of my own generation who might himself be a veteran of the Resistance. And by systematically declining to attend these jamborees, I was naturally only reinforcing the reputation I had already acquired for attractive humility; by (as it must have appeared) playing hard to get, merely encouraging others to extend ever more imploring invitations.

I had gone too far. My name, the name I'd tried so hard and for so long and until then so effectively to keep out of the public eye and ear, was well and truly 'made,' and in the weeks that followed the book's appearance I lived in a near-permanent state of dread, the most numbing I have ever known, a minute-by-minute terror that would bring on insomnia and beady sweats and bouts of physical, wrenching nausea. There was absolutely no one in whom I dared confide, no one for whom I *came first*, whom my confession would not have filled with disgust and incredulity. If I had murdered my wife in a fit of jealousy or had made off with the Mona Lisa, let's say, I could certainly have found it in myself to speak of my transgression all these many years later and probably too found a handful of sympathetic listeners. But the Holocaust! The Holocaust! For that – for that, on the campus of an American university – there could be no amnesty.

Nor was my fear any longer disproportionate to the very real risk that I was running. Two incidents occurred, a few months after the publication of *Either/Either*, which suggested to me that if I had once perhaps exaggerated the perils of promotion I was right to treat them seriously now.

The first was a relatively trivial matter. I had agreed to drive to New York one wintry Sunday with three of my colleagues from the department, Qualen, Basserman, and Gillingwater, to see a play that had just opened off-Broadway and was set on a university campus reportedly a lot like New Harbor.

But we arrived to find the performance sold out; and rebelling at the idea of heading back home empty-handed, so to speak, we decided to go see whatever movie was playing at the Thalia nearby. This turned out to be *To Be or Not to Be*, an amazingly tasteless and yet extremely funny Jack Benny comedy about a company of ham actors stranded in occupied Poland.

The incident occurred while we were on our way back to New Harbor, all of us a bit tipsy from too many cocktails at dinner. A fierce rainstorm combed the fantastically hued evening. The rain pelting down on Gillingwater's battered old Volkswagen from every angle made it quite claustrophobically snug; and feeling, in the seat beside him, as if I were peering at the smudgy, watery, yellowish world outside from underneath a great tight helmet or through some Gargantuan pair of goggles, I recall how obsessed I became by the maddening constancy with which the mechanical wipers, tracing and retracing, clockwise and counterclockwise, overlapping arcs across the windscreen in front of me, would contrive not quite, never quite, to jam in the middle. As I sat gazing thus at the beadlets of rain bombarding and beclouding the glass, my companions were quoting to each other some of the best lines from the movie in a glow of shared remembered laughter – and it was one of these that provoked the incident.

'Do you recall the scene,' burbled Basserman, whose knees I could feel pressing against the back of my seat, 'when the German officer is asked about Benny's Hamlet and replies, "What he did to Shakespeare we're doing to Poland!"?'

We all dutifully laughed again at this *bon mot*. Whereupon impossible foolish old Gillingwater turned to me and said, 'You know, Leo, that German officer reminds me of you.'

Suddenly, instinctively alert, I quietly asked what it was about him that reminded Herb of me.

'Why – what the Nazis did to Poland you've done to Yeats!'

I won't soon forget the scene: the rain, the garish gloom, the blurry little colonies of raindrops forming in the windscreen's four corners, the mocking, collusive laughter of Qualen and Basserman – laughter louder, in truth, than the joke deserved but pitched so in grudging acknowledgment that Gillingwater had for once excelled the standard of his usually pretty wretched witticisms.

I paused before speaking. Then I said somewhat brusquely, 'What on earth is that supposed to mean?'

Something, a coarse snap to my voice, caused the others to fall silent with parodic abruptness, and although I couldn't see either of the two seated in back of me I knew they had immediately glanced at each other with matching 'What's got into Leo?' expressions.

Gillingwater, fixing his eyes rigidly on the road ahead, not turning to reply to me, for more reason, I suspect, than merely that of keeping a straight course, began to mumble a clumsy excuse.

'I mean to say, in your book – in *Either/Either...*' (Herbert invariably mispronounced that title as *Eeether/Eyether* instead of *Eyether/Eeether*, a minuscule error and I'm sure an unintentional slight, but one hardly calculated to lighten a stony situation.)

Since that, however, seemed for the moment to be all there was going to be of his apology, it was Geoffrey Qualen who endeavored, not much less clumsily, as I felt, to rise to his defense. 'I imagine what Herb was trying to say was that you're one of the aggressive critics. You're like a Gestapo officer, you have ways' (which he accented, cod Germanically, as 'haf vays') 'of making a text talk. Heavens, Leo, don't be so uptight. He meant it as a compliment.'

I found myself forced in view of the circumstances to stand on a ceremony to which in truth I had no legitimate claim. 'I'm sorry, all of you,' I said, 'to appear so humorless. But, as you know, I lived through that whole period, which none of you did, and neither I nor my comrades ever felt able to treat the Gestapo as some kind of jokey simile.

Forgive me, but I'm afraid I still haven't learnt how.'

This hypocritical little speech finally succeeded in eliciting a thick muffled trailing apology from Herb, which was followed by a glumly strained silence that lasted more or less until we were driving through the calm leafy darkness of New Harbor's city center. And there again – in a way that, in spite of the obvious advantage to my position, I was starting to find quite frankly obscene – the exchange, when it duly made the rounds, simply added a fresh feather to a cap already overplumed, my stoic, circumspect memory of unhealed Resistance scars, which poor old Gillingwater's gaffe had obliged me to allude to after years of admirably discreet silence, providing yet another reason for enhaloing me.

The second incident, occurring some six months later, was an altogether more serious business. From Algiers of all places the Dean received an unsigned letter in French, short but to the point, which denounced me as having been a collaborationist in Paris during the Occupation. The Dean, who was no more than a nodding acquaintance of mine, didn't summon me into his office or ever speak to me in person about this letter. Instead, without any covering note, he forwarded it to me at my home address, its text defaced with, scribbled side by side, an enormous question mark and an even more enormous exclamation mark. Although the letter had been typed, its several childish solecisms and slightly less than secure syntax left me in no doubt at all as to its author's identity: it was from Louise.

I at once fired off my reply to the Dean. In this I carefully avoided any mention of my involvement with the Resistance, only, composedly, pointing out that, although all records relevant to my case were no doubt lost, I had been able to emigrate to the United States, which I couldn't have done so very easily had there been any reproach outstanding against me, had I been in short the collaborator of my accuser's fantasies. Perhaps, I added, there had arisen some confusion in his – my accuser's – memory with my father, who had indeed, it shamed me to confess, been censured for his intimate collaboration with the occupier. And I concluded by expressing the hope that the tenor and quality of my work in America rendered the untrustworthiness of such a charge so manifest as to warrant no serious consideration among intelligent men. I thanked the Dean for letting me see the letter which, unless I heard differently from him, I would prefer to destroy, since to accuse me behind my back of collaboration, and this to someone who could not conceivably verify or appreciate the facts, constituted a slanderous attack that left me quite helpless.

I received the very briefest of notes in response – 'Dear Léo, Your attitude is the only possible one to adopt. Of course you must destroy the letter. Yours,

Franklin' – and the subject was never raised again. Nor, it being the type of secret that is almost impossible to keep for any length of time from the grapevine of a university faculty like New Harbor, do I believe he ever spoke of it, even just as offhand gossip, to anyone. I would have known, with a vengeance, eventually.

But these two close shaves – the nightmarish fooleries of the first, the second's edgy civilized exchange – brought home to me with all the more force how precarious my position had become and I cursed myself for ever succumbing to the vainglorious temptation of writing and publishing such a book. It wasn't impossible, it was even likely now, that there would be other leakages, other awkward questions asked, other stray suggestive footnotes recollected, to draw the net ever more tightly around me. I couldn't live like this from day to day, gagging on every wormy fruit of my success. I don't pretend to be a novelist, an imaginer of plot and pathos. I can't, as vividly as I'd like, and hard as I try to, convey the awful endless apprehension that shivered through my being at the very thought of exposure. And if I described the incident in Herb's Volkswagen, the rainstorm, the wipers, the cramped and chilly but clammy interior, in detail more generous than that which I reserved for the, after all, graver harassment of the anonymous denunciation, it was because the sensation I had throughout this whole period was precisely of peering at the world from under a huge smothering helmet which had been clamped onto my overheated skull.

Then it was, out of that skull, that arose what I may call the idea of my life, an idea so grandiose, so sensational, I could feel my hair literally stand on end as I began to formulate it.

What was my purpose after all? To conjure an alibi – an alibi for three years of turpitude. An alibi that would persuade the world that, during those three years, thirty years ago, I had been *somewhere else*, intellectually if not in person (which would have been a hole-in-one beyond even my contrivance). An alibi that would say, ultimately: there can be no 'because' for a crime *I only appeared to commit*. And why could there be no 'because'? Why, because there was no 'why.'

The terrain was promising, the very ambiguities on which my alibi was to be erected were already hoveringly in the air; all I had to do was carry them out to their absurd and yet logical conclusion. The world, I felt certain, would meet me halfway. It was waiting for just such an alibi and amnesty, there were far, far more than I who would be thankful for it, who would eagerly hitch their fortunes to mine – as gamblers at a roulette table, whatever confidence they might once have professed in the infallibility of their own systems, will always pragmatically defer to a winner's success and gratefully trust their chips to the same lucky number as he has his. It was never going to be, plausibly, a matter of subverting, of reversing facts. Nothing can ever be subverted, nothing reversed – like a lead-weighted doll, it will always right itself in the end. It was a matter, rather, of going forth, not back, of taking the thing, recklessly, unflinchingly, as far as it could go, of reinterpreting history itself, doing what not even God can do: altering the past.

Voilà. I was one of the most eminent critics in the United States. I had disciples aplenty, who (the cliché says it best) hung on my every word. I was already poised to become the jewel of the country's most prestigious Ivy League institution. And one not unexpected effect of my first book was the paradox of its having repudiated the primacy of the Author in order to establish its own author's name. Not unexpected, because it was a fundamental rule of the game that as a radical theorist I was playing with my readers. I knew that they knew and they knew that I knew that for my book to exert the influence it so obviously sought to exert it alone had to pretend to be free of all those riddling equivocations and honeycombed voids that it claimed to detect in the texts on which it passed comment. It alone had to be read and interpreted as its author meant it to be read and interpreted *and no other way* – thereby confounding the very principle of the death of the Author and the plurality of possible readings that it was also expounding. For, after all, if I had really believed in the death of the Author, why should I have bothered to ensure that my name appear on the jacket of my book?

And one day I was musing in this vein when the idea came to me. What, I thought, was to prevent me from *truly* killing the Author, and along with Him one author in particular whom I despised above all others and whom I longed to liquidate, in the picturesque military formula, with extreme prejudice? A clever man, said Laubreaux, can argue anything if he sets his mind to it. Very well, very well, I would engineer the death of the Author, his final solution, his elimination from the Text of the world. With the ruthless dazzling irrefutable logic of which I had become the master I would deny not merely the primacy but the very existence of the Author – *and therefore deny the very existence of Hermes.* I would argue that authorial presence had to be redefined as an absence – *and therefore that Hermes' authorial presence had to be redefined as an absence.* That, far from there being a single privileged interpretation for every text, there existed no text that permitted interpretation on any level whatsoever – *and therefore no text of Hermes that permitted interpretation on any level whatsoever.* That, since all texts were self-referential entities, the words that articulated them, and that only ever connected with other words, could never be made to reflect a 'real' world outside of those texts – *and therefore that none of Hermes' words could ever be made to reflect a real world outside of his texts.* That, from a theoretical viewpoint, considerations of the actual and historical existence of a writer were an utter waste of time – *and therefore that considerations of Hermes' actual and historical existence were an utter waste of time.* That, when subject to the closest analysis, to the most rigorous exercise of decipherment, every text could be shown infallibly to unmask and undermine the ideology that it appeared to be endorsing – *and therefore that Hermes' texts could be shown infallibly to unmask and undermine the Nazi ideology that they appeared to be endorsing.* That, finally, at the most profound level of such analysis, all meaning, all intelligibility, all possibility of interpretation, would dissolve into a rattle of disconnected voices, an infinite regression of empty linguistic signs – this would be, of every text, *and therefore of every text of Hermes*, the terminus, the last stop before the abyss, what I elected to call, in an inspiration that delighted me, its aporia.

There, in the future principles of the Theory, was my alibi. Naturally, if the book in which I planned to set these principles forth were to no more than match the success of *Either/Either* – and I couldn't know then how immeasurably greater a triumph was to be reserved for *The Vicious Spiral* – it would take me one crucial step closer to my apotheosis and hence my probable exposure as a Nazi collaborator. At the same time, however, and here was the peculiar beauty of my stratagem, it would exonerate me – both retroactively and in advance, so to speak – of precisely those offenses that the afterglow of its publication risked once for all bringing to the light.

It wasn't going to be child's play, of that I was well aware. It wasn't going to be easy to destigmatize myself, *ex post facto*, with what after all was a work of pure theory. I wasn't so gullible as to suppose that my book would represent the kind of evidence likely to stand up in a court of law. Awaiting me, whatever the outcome, was a *mauvais quart d'heure* that I would have to brace myself to confront and numb myself to endure. At the very least, the special aura which had been mine, with which I had been invested as a scholar and critic, would have evaporated for ever.

In this regard, though, I was less concerned with my opponents, and with what they might have to say, than with my disciples, my erstwhile champions, who, as I feared, were unlikely soon, perhaps ever, to forgive my youthful indiscretions; who would shrink not only from me but from the henceforth tainted theoretical apparatus that, like a duelist choosing the weapon in which he is most practiced, I had brought to bear upon my defense.

Yet of all the things in the world that the lemming-like *genus* of academic mediocrity takes to its collective heart it holds none more dear than a doctrine, a catechism, a preprogrammed system, whose rules it has only to learn by rote then commit to memory – and, as the ultimate authority of that doctrine, a now gentle, now ruthless lawgiver, now father-figure, now führer, with thunderbolts poking out of his breast-pocket like fountain pens. Among these many disciples of mine, I had, I was confident, more than a fair share of lumbering nonentities incapable of stringing a couple of literate sentences together and for whom criticism was a form of intellectual red tape, its every tiny and nondescript insight spelt out in triplicate, its tumorous propagation of clotted clauses and subclauses vainly struggling to animate and articulate the semblance of a coherent argument. It was these nonentities, I knew, on whom I could best rely, it was they who would seek cynical advantage to themselves in marching to my tune, exploiting my new and I hoped fashionable doctrine as a means of rescuing their careers from the thick gray fog of middlingness in which they had become stalled. There were those, too, who would delight in using it as a grid by which they could interpret the world without ever having to trouble their own intellects, without ever having to think for themselves – and best of all feel invigoratingly rebellious, heretical, and iconoclastic in doing so. And there were others who were born to be courtiers and in whose scraping and train-bearing psychology the thrill of sitting at a master's feet was of infinitely greater significance than what it was those feet might have been made of. I could already anticipate how disciples such as these, mortally afraid that the disgrace of the father would be visited upon his too credulous sons and daughters, would rush to my defense, would frantically set about interpreting my old articles in the light of my new theories. And I even managed to excavate from my own dim recollection of those articles the odd passage whose syntactical ambiguity could be held up as more or less conclusive proof that its superficial sense had indeed been ingeniously contrived with the dual purpose of deceiving my Nazi masters while directing the more perceptive reader toward a whole other, latent sense, the sense of a covert attack that I had courageously mounted against the abhorrent ideology of which I appeared to be the most servile of drudges.

As a solution, it was always going to be a compromise, one from which my reputation could never hope to emerge intact. The alternatives, though, were simply unimaginable. Even if such self-abasement were possible at this stage of my professional life, I could not revert to the seedy anonymity of Raphaël's bookstore or any such equivalent; nor, naturally, could I defend the indefensible. In any event, I told myself, it all might never happen.

I wrote *The Vicious Spiral* with for me astounding speed, in the heat of that inspiration which I had so often dismissed as a critical concept, wrote it by hand on the lined pages of a rising pile of exercise jotters, a fact that encouraged me to polish my style beyond what I'd been generally accustomed to settle for – it was as if, from its very first draft, I felt that each of its sentences had to justify its having been underlined even before it was written. Hence, no doubt, the stately tread of its prose and the almost mathematical elegance and intricacy of its scintillescent web of ideas (all thought aspires to mathematics as, said Pater, all art aspires to music). The entire work was completed in a matter of seven months, and I had, as you may suppose, no problem whatever in persuading the New Harbor Press to accept it for immediate publication.

The plan had been laid, and to an extent its success depended on the eventual success of the book itself. At the same time I was scarcely angling for any attention beyond the academic world, merely the scholar's usual *succès d'estime*, the intimate and confidential approbation of the happy few. So it was with incredulous horror that I saw it turn into a publishing phenomenon, a triumph that far exceeded my most unbridled fantasies and that I couldn't help perceiving as the first real golden nail in my coffin.

I became famous. I even became wealthy after a fashion, for *The Vicious Spiral* briefly entered the *New York Times*'s bestseller list – never rising above the lower end of the scale, to be sure, and generally assumed to have had significantly more purchasers than it ever had readers, but in there nevertheless. My delirious publisher began to forward reviews and articles and letters, personal letters – fan mail! – in thick unreadable bundles. And the extravagant speculations that I had designed with the sole purpose of exculpating myself had curdled into the Theory. The Theory! A tidal wave, it engulfed one campus after another, it split in two as many faculties as the Dreyfus affair had split families at the turn of the century, it engendered the most fatally irreconcilable of either/ors: one was either for it or against it, with no possible halfway house. I had to stand by helpless as economic journalists referred to a Theory of Wall Street, sports columnists applied it to the World Series, fashion editors to *prêt-à-porter* collections. It entered the dictionary and the language. Johnny Carson even made a crack about it on *The Tonight Show*. And, a mere thirty months after the publication of the book, horribly sooner, then, than I had expected anything of the kind to develop, Astrid Hunneker came to me to announce her intention of writing the history, authorized or unauthorized, of my life.

When she told me what it was she meant to do, my initial instinct was to look at my watch. This, merely a reflex on my part, an unfortunately timed one as I realized at once, she completely misunderstood. The smiling defiance tempered by apprehension with which she had announced her news to me swiftly drained from her features to be replaced by a moue of sulky disgruntlement. She was galled, nonplussed too, as I could see, that I had chosen no less than the crucial point in our interview, that at which she had played her trump card, to display what she presumably interpreted as my rude, fidgety impatience with her. Yet how could I convey to her that what I sought on my watch face was not the time but, as it were, time; that what I saw and all I saw (insofar as I saw anything at all) were the second and minute hands executing their immemorial hare-and-tortoise pursuit around the dial, the former advancing at a strictly measured pace, the latter, all wily invisible stealth, regularly outdistancing it from pit stop to pit stop? How was she to know that I had been waiting nearly seventeen years for someone to say to me what she had just said – for it, for this circumstance, to come about, as if it were finally its 'turn'? And how could I tell her that I had already made up my mind, possibly as late as at the very second she disclosed her project to me but already nevertheless, to forge ahead on my own? When things have to be said, they have to be said. Eventually they have to be said.

'Do I take it, Professor Sfax,' she asked in a tone suggesting that her previous temerity had once more got the upper hand, 'that your reservations –'

'Oh but, you see, I have no reservations,' I replied, smiling for the first time since my gaffe. 'On the contrary, I approve – for all that *that's* worth.'

Now she could barely credit how exorbitantly the situation seemed to have swung in her favor. 'So you won't, I mean to say, you won't put any obstacles in my way?'

I assured her I would lend every assistance that could reasonably be expected of me – I believe in diplomacy and, if occasion permit, tolerance – and would even compose a short preliminary text to aid her in her research. But I felt bound to warn her in the same breath that there was little enough I *could* do, that in particular most of the data relating to an early period of my life could no longer be appreciated or verified, too much of the relevant documentation having been lost. It was far too soon in any event to worry about all that. Understandably, she had preferred to speak to me first before even approaching a publishing house, and I may as well admit, although I naturally forbore to say so to her, that at this precocious stage of its development the entire enterprise struck me as having a very moot future indeed.

It was as I accompanied her to my office door that I cast my famously mild eyes over her fair, bony, very patrician, very 'East Coast,' and altogether pretty face, fringed as by the pasteboard curtain sashes of a toy theater by a tangle of reddish-brown hair.

'You realize,' I said, smiling still, 'that you will never *get* me? Nobody ever has.'

Now it was her turn to smile, toothily, almost girlishly – a smile as spontaneous and unpremeditated as a blush.

'Didn't you know I sculpted?' she suddenly asked, as if it somehow 'showed,' for how I was otherwise supposed to know such a thing I couldn't imagine.

'No – really?'

'Only figurative stuff, I'm afraid. Heads, mostly. But they do say I'm very strong on likenesses. I mean to capture yours – if you'll let me.'

I made the primly strategic reply that first it would be for a publisher to let her – 'Where there's a will there's a way,' I murmured, '– or rather, where there's a way there's a will.'

She laughed; then, with a handshake, we said goodbye.

I returned to my desk to think over this strange little scene. I looked again at my watch, but this time just to see the time. Her appointment had been at five and it was by a minute gone half-past. So – it had taken only half-an-hour to cast the die. And it was a sculptress who cast it. A sculptress? Is everyone fated to have at least one sculptress in their life? Astrid! Her very name was a signifier of the 'creative' in all its poignant horror. No, truly no, I couldn't entrust my head to her.

I checked that I had no more appointments that afternoon and, satisfied that the rest of the day was mine to do with as I pleased, I switched on my Apple Mac computer. I opened a new file, to which I gave the password *Hermes*, and for a good five or six minutes sat there staring at the screen, the blank white screen-page, until at last I set to typing (I'm a two-finger man, basically – or even one, the left forefinger serving as not much more than the right's assistant, intervening, like the less agile half of a tennis doubles partnership, to bag an occasional comma or apostrophe) the ninety-nine pages that you have just been reading.

It was two months after this, in the February of the following year, that Astrid Hunneker telephoned me with the great news. Offering the new-minted modishness of her subject as collateral, she had beyond all expectation successfully approached a publisher, which was neither my own New Harbor nor the whimsical little press that had brought out her dissertation but some major New York house with offices on Fifth Avenue. This publisher was keen enough on the prospect of an authorized biography of the celebrated Léopold Sfax to have already offered her a contract, in middling five figures no less, and, as she informed me with all the blithe heartlessness of youth, to have encouraged her to get going on it at once for fear the bloom be off the rose, the meteor of my celebrity subside, before publication day. She planned, she told me, to commute between her parents' Manhattan town house – which I gathered was somewhere on the city's Upper East Side – and New Harbor, where she would be spending most of her time in the Ruggles and sharing an apartment with Ralph MacMahon, who had introduced her to the joys of the Theory and was still struggling to complete his interminable thesis.

The scheme which Astrid had devised for us was for her to conduct a series of taped interviews with me, the information gained therein assisting her to find her way about the Paris of my childhood and youth, where, flush with her five-figure advance, she hoped to travel in the early summer. In the first instance I fell in with this program. But I did warn her that, because of faculty commitments that simply wouldn't permit so concentrated a blitz on my time, I could not possibly make myself available during the six or seven consecutive days that she ideally sought from me. I didn't reveal my other and, as you may believe, more imperative motive for fending her off, which was that I hadn't the slightest intention of sitting down with her in my office and, a tape-recorder eavesdropping on my every word, either telling the whole truth or else perjuring myself about my life.

Now that it had come to this pass, now that it was finally its 'turn,' I felt hopelessly unprepared, overtaken by events, frantic for some delaying tactic that would give me time to think. It may surprise the reader that, having written *The Vicious Spiral* for exactly the eventuality that had presented itself, I should thus recoil from baldly confronting the situation and carrying my guilt before me as lightly as I could. But too much had happened too fast, and to be honest I had always expected the assault when it came to arrive from France, from some unknown, disinterested, and more or less abstract quarter with which I might be spared any direct and personal confrontation. In any case, no mental projection of a future event, even if accurate to the very last degree, can ever precapture the thud of the blow when it has been delivered at long last.

There was, as well, a problem that I had not foreseen. Since, if it were to save my skin, *The Vicious Spiral* would have to lay down, clearly and dogmatically, a set of hypotheses that were bound to meet with some initial resistance, I found that I had on occasion slipped into an idiom far less suave, far more aggressive and violent, than I had ever employed in the past. To describe the sort of treatment I believed lay in store for all the old outmoded critical habits and practices that my own and my followers' work would sweep away for ever, I had used words, crazily, irresponsibly, as I realize now, like 'rape' and 'destroy' and 'invade' and 'exterminate,' and I even went so far as to refer to certain of the concepts in the book as 'totalizing and potentially totalitarian.' And this uncharacteristic intemperance of language had had the awkward effect of causing the Theory's enemies to stand their ground, to dig in, with more than one hostile commentator claiming that it was fundamentally fascistic in nature, shot through with ideological nihilism and amorality. To my especial horror, an important critic, a professor of literature at Harvard whom I'd always thought of as my ally and friend, wrote in his review of the book that, I quote, 'there is nothing in the so-called Theory that could serve as a basis, *for example*, for repudiating, and so providing an ethical critique, of Nazism.' The emphasis is mine: for I knew that were the revelations of my past to surface on this crest of animosity I could not, nor could my work, survive.

My original intention, therefore, had been to postpone indefinitely, by making this excuse and that, the first groundbreaking session with Astrid that she was already begging me to grant her. But I felt it politic after all to cooperate with her as far as I dared, and we met for a couple of hours one afternoon in my office where I managed to maneuver our conversation almost entirely toward our eventual *modus operandi*, toward the need to define and establish a line of action that we might adopt in the future, and away from anything that could have proved difficult for me to foil. We also chatted idly about the Theory and compared notes on the classic English detective novels which she seemed to devour on an almost daily basis.

That she was likely to feel restless and thwarted after so unproductive a start I had anticipated. So, as she was leaving, without having teased out of me a precise date for our next appointment, I handed over to her the twenty-page account of my life that I had typed out on my computer specifically for this purpose and hoped she would construe as a special privilege to her, the token and trophy of my readiness to cooperate. It was very much the orthodox version, but leavened all the same by the froth of a 'personal touch,' by an airy whimsicality of tone – in the description, notably, of a curious little crisis of identity at my grandfather's graveside. It also laid especial emphasis on my friendship with Raphaël and his wife, whom I could find no good reason for her not to go see, if either of them still chanced to be alive. (Although hardly an irregular visitor to

New York myself, I had never thought to remake contact with them, nor, in spite of my celebrity, had they with me.) In the meantime I took the positive course and went about my life and business as before, giving classes, meeting with my graduate students, making notes for some as yet vaguely defined new project that I had.

Then something fantastical happened in New Harbor, something that brought my work as it brought the whole routine of the faculty to a jarring halt. Herb Gillingwater was murdered!

I must have been among the very last to hear of it. Feeling the onset of a flushed, sore-throaty 'flu that I was at once reassured was 'going around,' I had canceled all my appointments and taken my work home with me. When in the late afternoon the telephone call came through from a breathless, shaken, incredulous Qualen – albeit still, at some level of his being, detectably enchanted to be the bearer of news as exciting as it was shocking – I was lying stretched out on a sofa with Proust in my hand and gazing distractedly through my tall study window at the snow-hemmed eaves and cornices of the campus buildings, which looked in the dusk and in the distance rather like shadows in white negative.

It appears that, on the day before, without notifying his students that he planned to do so, Gillingwater had missed first his two o'clock then his four o'clock class; nor did he subsequently ring in or answer his own telephone. Although he lived alone, and was regarded as chronically feckless in domestic matters, no one had felt the urge to take fright until one of the department secretaries, a near-neighbor of his, had called at his house on her way home the following evening, had noticed that his daily newspaper was lying on the porch where it had been delivered in the morning, had vainly rung his doorbell, found the door unlocked, stepped in, and all but tripped over poor old Herb's body. His skull had been shattered; next to it, clearly the crime's blunt instrument, lay an absurd bronze bust of Shakespeare that he had bought in some tourist trap in Stratford-upon-Avon and that all of us had ribbed him about, now smeared with his blood and brains.

As it happens, I'd received, and due to the 'flu that I sensed coming on had already declined, an invitation to dinner that evening at the Qualens'; and when Geoffrey had completed his grisly narrative I asked him if under the circumstances I might be permitted after all to accept. Qualen, who was as eager to talk the extraordinary thing through as I was myself, told me to come right over – he lived on the far side of town so that I had to walk right across the campus area where a flotilla of police cars was already parked outside the Dean's offices.

After paying due obeisance to this unmitigated tragedy, to what the loss of our friend meant to us, our talk at the dinner table was naturally of little else but the motivation for so very meaningless, to all appearances meaningless, a crime. We had next to no solid information to chew on and could only for the moment imagine that Herb had surprised some intruder, since there was no other reason that any of us could fathom for the killing of quite the most harmless man in the world, a man as free of personal ambition as he was of a personal fortune, who had no enemies and so far as anyone knew no close relatives, and whose sexual life was a complete conundrum – if indeed it existed at all, which most of us had always doubted. Herb, in short, had never harmed a living creature, and it was beyond us why any living creature should have harmed him.

Yet there had been no intruder. The precise facts of the case were hard to come by, but in the course of the next week it became common knowledge about the faculty that nothing had been stolen from Herb's house and that there was no indication whatever that he had struggled with his assailant. In fact, his own crumpled body apart, the sole off-key element in what had been, from what we heard, a tableau of uncanny stillness and normality was a blot of port on the carpet which the poor secretary who discovered him had mistaken for more of his blood. Clearly Herb had had no cause not to open his front door to his killer nor invite him to come in; and he was brained for his pains when about to pour out two glasses of the old English port wine that, unconditional Anglophile as he was, he would always, slightly complacently, offer his visitors. It was also bruited about that he had been struck down from in front and so must have realized what was going to happen to him; and, to general amazement that the secret had been kept so well and for so long, that he had worn a toupee.

I have to say that it was that one particular detail which haunted me – not the toupee, of course, but the idea that Herb had laid eyes on this individual just as he was on the point of felling him, probably even seen the bust of Shakespeare raised above his own head. Was his brain, in its ultimate instant of cognition, its last gasp of conscious sensation, still capable of registering that someone, a friend no doubt, an acquaintance at the least, was about to smash it into pulp? The notion of that moment – quite Dostoevskian, I thought, in its existential terror – when poor old Herb had still perhaps time enough to comprehend that he was about to be murdered and time to comprehend too that he would go to his death without knowing why he was being murdered, was almost more intolerable to me than the fact itself of the crime.

*

Astrid, I would later learn from her, had been out of town when it occurred. Evidently, though, it had been brazenly run in all the New York tabloids – in a country where serial killers have to take care not to trespass on each other's territory, there being so awfully many of them, the murder of an elderly don in his own library, the 'fact,' as even the more serious newspapers typically announced, that he had been a pillar of the famous Theory (!), the added piquancy of a spilt decanter of port and a lethal bust of Shakespeare, had a fruitily nostalgic, Agatha Christieish flavor to it which must have drawn out the amateur sleuth that slumbers in every reporter. And, as I fully expected her to do, given her fascination with the genre, she had at once come haring back to New Harbor.

It was a series of messages left on my answering machine, which I let go unreturned, that apprised me of her presence on the campus. She refused, however, to take a hint. One evening, about four or five days after Herb's body had been discovered, my doorbell rang and there she impeccably stood, lavish with apologies for daring to bother me at home and assurances that she hadn't come to plague me with inopportune queries on our work together. She had been moved and shaken by the death of her old teacher and simply wanted to know, she said, whether any clue to the mystery or any glimmering of its solution had meanwhile emerged that she hadn't been able to cull from the press coverage or else from what Ralph could tell her. She was brimming with ideas on the affair – ideas, those at least she felt at liberty to confide to me, that like her thesis were as long on ingenuity as they were short on coherence – and she seemed to be hoping that I might possess some inside knowledge denied her, an illusion I soon corrected. Actually, it was she who gave me a fact I hadn't known – that an FBI detective had been assigned to the case and was already prowling about the campus.

As life in New Harbor progressively settled on a truce of, if not normality, then an uneasy semi-normality, no significant clues having as yet been unearthed on the identity of Herb's murderer and everyone still making light of a vague but quite perceptible and pervasive jumpiness, I began to hear more and more of this agent – his name I learned was Brophy – from colleagues of mine whom he had interviewed; and he eventually found his way to my own office.

I had already been forewarned by those who had spoken to him not to expect anything very stagy or cloak-and-daggerish. And, as it turned out, he was a pleasantly nondescript fellow in, at a guess, his early forties, faintly florid in complexion, wearing a rather heavy old-fashioned style of horn-rimmed spectacles and a haircut too short, trim, and close-cropped about the ears for a head as large and foursquare as his was. He addressed me with a deference I thought unusual in one of his type, but, coming in the wake of so many identical sessions, our interview was as cruelly brief as a failed audition. After a preliminary round establishing that Herb had been a friend of mine as well as a colleague, and that I had last properly seen and spoken to him a few weeks previously, it essentially boiled down to the question of whether I knew of any reason why someone might have chosen to murder him.

I replied that there the mystery was complete. Not perhaps New Harbor's foremost scholar, intellectually rather local, and sometimes a bit of a joke, Herb was a man whose life was an open book if anyone's was, with no shadow on his character, no dim unsavory recess that any of us were aware of in his past, nothing at all that might, in short, have 'caught up with him.' Personally speaking, I said truthfully, I had been extremely fond of Herb, as had everyone I knew who had known him.

Brophy responded to my concise little summation of Herb's human qualities with a patient Spartan smile, so far the last thing I expected from him that I couldn't resist asking what had prompted it.

He leaned back confidently in his chair. 'You see, Professor Sfax, it's this way. You are just about the last of Herbert Gillingwater's friends I have had to talk to' – at this he drew a small yellow scratch pad from his hip pocket, waved it at me, and explained almost bashfully, 'I conduct these things in alphabetical order, you understand, not in order of, well, eminence,' as if I might have taken offence at being considered of such low priority – 'and you've just said to me exactly, but *exactly*, what everybody else did. Herb Gillingwater was a nice, sweet, innocent man, with no money to steal, no wife to seduce, no skeletons to rattle, and not an enemy in the world.'

'But it *is* all exactly so,' I replied helplessly. 'Herb *had* no enemies. Everybody liked him.'

'Professor,' he said, 'somebody didn't. Somebody *really* didn't like good old Herb.'

I was surprised by such untimely flippancy and gave him a penetrating look that led him to add: 'I apologize. I shouldn't have spoken like that about a friend of yours who has just been murdered. But I have to say, I've never come up against a brick wall as blank as this. If I were paranoid I would begin to think all of you were conspiring to make me believe there could have been no earthly reason for wanting Herbert Gillingwater out of the way. And possibly,' he added, 'I was hoping for something more enlightening from you...'

I replied that I didn't follow his meaning. He shyly smiled. 'What I'm saying, Professor Sfax, is that I'm actually something of an admirer of yours. Oh' – to what I fear was the involuntary snub of my own raised eyebrows – 'I wouldn't claim to understand everything you write – no more than one idea per page – *at most* – still, you know, I find it all does make for a very stimulating read. Especially with that very particular style that you have. And I suppose I was hoping,' here his tone became half-humorous, 'that you, the father of the Theory – well, that you might have come out with a theory or two on this business.'

'Ah, Mr Brophy,' I murmured with a flattered smile, 'there are theories and theories. And then there is the Theory.'

He laughed; then said, 'I wonder if you would mind,' and from his neat black briefcase pulled out a copy of *The Vicious Spiral*, which he asked me to inscribe. I did so, at the same time making some lamebrained pleasantry about the cunning with which he had thus obtained a sample of my handwriting; and, with a promise on my part to contact him if anything should subsequently occur to me that might shed light on the affair, the interview ended.

Herb's funeral, which was held three days later in the City Burial Ground, was in its way a really quite affecting ceremony and well attended by even distant acquaintances of his in the faculty, if not by the veiled enigmatic unidentified woman in black on whose presence some of his former colleagues had jovially and rather tastelessly wagered. As far as I could see, there were no unknown mourners at all.

Brophy was there, standing a little way apart from the university faction; Astrid too, I noticed, looking lusciously chic and solemn. We exchanged a word or two after it was over and agreed to meet for a lengthy session two days thence.

We met at my home, where I spoke to her of my childhood, mostly, and in wholly peaceful conscience, as it struck me as safe enough ground for biographical extrapolation. I fleshed out those details on my family, and in particular on the swords that my grandfather had so unwisely crossed with Zola at the time of the Dreyfus trial, of which she was already in possession from my little written chronicle. And in truth, if the conversation more than once drifted off the subject, it was I who had to reverse it back onto the relevant track whenever Astrid started distractedly musing aloud about Herb's killing. She had frequently had cause to wonder, she told me, whether such on the surface motiveless and 'perfect' but underneath no doubt all too deviously driven crimes had ever been committed outside of the detective fiction to which she was addicted – I had the impression that she'd have been over the moon, in her own macabre seventh heaven, had poor old Gillingwater been found dead in some hermetically sealed and windowless room!

She also mentioned to me, without a hint of coquetry, when I thought to ask 'after him,' that Ralph and she had had a furious row over her coming to see me in this way at my home and admitted, for whatever I cared to make of it, that half in love with me while she was still on campus she had indeed been dogging my path as I suspected. To my surprise I was growing to like her, to like the bold unhedged manner in which she made such a potentially delicate confession, the fact that she had discarded most of her arch physical affectations and had learned to talk with me and just be with me without my feeling either that I was being asked to accord her a sham equality of rank or the indulgence due to the 'groupie.' I even started to fancy that a solution to my problem with her and her accursed biography might lie in our getting to know each other very much better.

However, only a week later these and all such speculations were brought to a premature end. I was at home in my study one midday when I received a phone call from her. Instead of the poised and slightly peppery Astrid I had come to know she sounded very breathy and overwrought, as if she were cupping her hand protectively over the receiver. Yet she insisted that she was quite alone in the apartment she and Ralph shared and I could hear the faint and silvery rustle of recorded harpsichord music in the background. This apartment was just a couple of blocks away from the Wannabe, a local coffee house and student hang-out, where she asked me if I would meet her at once – it was also just a ten-minute stroll from my home.

At once I could not, and told her so; and when I then inquired whether her problem was of a sufficiently urgent nature to distract me from work that assuredly was, she answered that a crucial, a *really, really* significant, clue to the murder had come to her. Something I had mentioned about Herb at our last session together (she would not say what over the phone) had been nagging at her all week, it had at last clicked, to use her word, that morning, and she wanted to make doubly certain of it before bearing it in triumph to Brophy. It all seemed to me a childish and melodramatic rigmarole, and I marveled at how quickly and thoroughly her head could be turned by such whimsies; but she did insist, and I agreed to meet her at the Wannabe an hour later.

Although I was almost ten minutes late, Astrid herself, to my intense surprise and irritation, was not yet there when I arrived. The café was crowded; providentially, though, one of the booths was just at that instant being vacated. Under the collective scrutiny of a bemused and hushed clientèle, which had never seen me in the Wannabe before and appeared to find the spectacle absolutely mind-boggling, and confident that no student would either care or dare to sit beside the father of the Theory, I immediately claimed it and ordered a hot chocolate.

On the wall directly opposite me was a blackboard with all the Wannabe's regular fare chalked across it and, conveniently above that, a huge round Mickey Mouse clock dial which I had only to look up at from my chocolate to remind myself, minute by minute, just how cavalier Astrid was being about punctuality, the more so in view of the urgency she had invested in our appointment.

Ten minutes passed. Could she *have* been punctual, I began to wonder, but left again before I arrived, in just the state of exasperation I myself was in at present? It seemed hardly likely. Only a few weeks before, her attitude to me had been one of blushing and still easily embarrassed deference and I couldn't credit that her more recent informality of manner had already reached the stage where she felt she could take me for granted. But ten more minutes went by: she was now a half-hour late, and I didn't know how much longer I could sit in front of my empty chocolate cup. If I knew her telephone number, I said to myself, I might ring – when I remembered that I did at least know her address, that it was close by, and that I could call there before returning home.

I asked for the check; then, aware of being caught again in a crossfire of stares that were none the wiser than when I had arrived, I left the Wannabe and almost at once collided with Ralph MacMahon. Wheeling a bicycle at his side, he was on his way home. He didn't greet me so much as coolly acknowledge my existence, and the ice was no nearer breaking when I told him where I was going. Fortunately the apartment was a very short walk across the street, so we had neither the time nor the obligation to make much in the way of small talk.

Astrid and he lived on the first floor of a two-story redbrick building. Ralph parked his bike on the landing and let himself into the apartment, negligently leaving the door ajar that I should follow. Inside, in a narrow hallway, and with the yawning torpor of a stripper, he let his extravagantly quilted windbreaker slide off his footballer's shoulders onto the floor and called out Astrid's name. There was no answer. I stood for a moment, uncertain what to do next, while he strode into the kitchen, pulled a can of beer from the icebox, sprang it open, and took a luxuriously long deep swig. Then, cloddishly, almost as if he were quite deliberately barging against the furniture, he marched into what I'd already seen through its half-open door to be a messy parlor-cum-studio and with a juddery abruptness came to a sudden silent halt. I went in after him. Along the far wall of the room was a sofa over which a filthy, paint-streaked dustsheet had been thrown, and Astrid must have been sitting side-saddle on one of its arms, dangling her legs as she would, like a marionette's, when she was struck. Her body – she was wearing some sort of folksy embroidered ankle-length smock or pinafore – was splayed at a weird warped angle aslant the sofa, her legs, propped against its back, indecently sliced the air like an open pair of scissors. Her face, although unendurable in its agony, was wholly unblemished; but visible under hair so long it trailed the carpet was a crack in her skull like the squashed-in dome of a boiled egg. Beside her head, lying as near to it as if whispering in its ear, was another head, a sculpted terracotta bust; and even though its nose had been broken by the impact, and Astrid's talent as a sculptress was no more than that of a decent amateur, there could be no doubt at all that that second head was mine.

She had been modeling my head from memory, it transpired, perhaps also from the photograph of me on the jacket flap of *The Vicious Spiral*, a copy of which stood on the mantelpiece where one might have expected to find a candlestick or someone's framed snapshot. It was from Brophy that I learned this, and a lot else besides. He had questioned Ralph, who owned quite freely to the fact that tensions between himself and Astrid had recently arisen from her closer association with me. And she, it seemed, had also mentioned to Ralph, in as tantalizingly unspecific a fashion as to myself, her discovery of a clue to Herb's killing – though, alas, neither by the racking of my brain nor by Brophy's ransacking of their apartment was the least trace of this clue exhumed.

It was all too patent that Astrid had been 'onto something,' that her 'hunch' had been genuine enough, that she had been murdered in her turn on account of it. I felt culpably that her life might have been saved had I agreed to meet her at the Wannabe at once, as she had asked me, and not kept her waiting that fatal hour, and the question that exercised Brophy, since Ralph had an alibi of sorts, having been vaguely observed on the football field where he claimed he had been practising all afternoon, was when Astrid had divulged her secret to a third party, the most interested of all, Herb's murderer.

As can easily be imagined, this second crime, arriving so soon after the first, reanimated all the stir its predecessor had caused, and then some. The tabloids positively gloated over so very outré and perverse a serial killer, whom they naturally baptized 'The Bust Man,' while even the serious press found it hard to resist flying the lyrical flag. 'The Graves of Academe,' I recall, was one unsightly headline that leered at us all from the newsstands. 'Steeped in blood as it once was in tradition, fear now stalks the shady avenues and ivied halls of beautiful New Harbor...' – that was the sort of tripe we had to put up with. And one faintly comical side effect to the affair was that those few locals who happened to own just the sort of bust that had been twice employed by the killer, and who therefore felt themselves to be especially vulnerable to his lunatically artistic aggressions, had hurriedly stowed these away in their cellars or happily parted with them at knockdown prices.

The effect on my own life was immediate and lamentable, my name and fame having been revived in the way and at the time I would have chosen last. Nothing in Brophy's very lax and lenient questioning of me prepared me for the malignity of the interrogations to which I was subjected by journalists who patently knew little of me beyond that name and fame and for whom I was just some bread-and-butter celebrity caught up in a juicy scandal. And it was all the worse when they *had* done their homework. On my own doorstep one pushy young man from the *Village Voice* quoted back at me my phrase on death as a displaced name for a linguistic predicament and inquired in a sarcastically sober-sided tone whether I, the Theorist, had a theory as to who might have been responsible for these two regrettable linguistic predicaments that had just arisen in New Harbor. Alarmed to see me badgered so, the Dean finally suggested that I take a couple of weeks leave from the faculty until it should blow over, and even offered me use of a cottage he and his wife had on the Cape, two gifts I was grateful to accept. I packed a few essentials and left the very next day.

The vacation I spent in Truro I spent entirely alone, walking under clear high skies and reading whatever chanced to appeal to me in the Dean's modest library and most of all thinking, thinking about everything that had occurred, about Astrid's death and what it had meant to me. There was of course a heaven-sent something about this death that I could not conceal from myself, that indeed, and in spite of myself, had stayed uppermost in my mind throughout the entire ordeal. She would not now write my biography, she would not travel to Paris to nose about in my past, and many years might elapse before someone else had the same bright idea. I couldn't pretend that this was not a source of colossal relief to me, that a burden had not been removed which allowed me to breathe again. On the other hand I would never be able to shake the image, as on some vulgar book jacket, of her body splayed over the sofa, her head grazing the floor, and her limbs all askew. It hunted me down wherever, on the lonely unattended beach, inside a movie theater, or on the page of a book, I sought to escape it; and I knew that it was a price more terrible than any I would have been prepared to exact for my own security.

In the end I didn't stick out the whole two weeks in Truro but returned to New Harbor after just ten days, refreshed, calmer, even slightly bored, and as primed as I was likely ever to be for the old inevitable routine of meetings and classes and seminars.

I felt I had to devote my first day back to answering the mail that had accumulated in my absence, and I thought too to ring Brophy to find out whether there was any development in the case I ought to be told about – if they had ever run it, the local Truro rags had already lost interest in the story by the time I arrived. Brophy had nothing at all fresh to offer me, though. Without Astrid's clue, which needless to say I still couldn't remember having given her, his investigation was at an impasse. In practical terms, he had no one left to question.

I had picked up the bundle of mail in the morning to take home with me, but returned to the office late in the afternoon to collect a few papers that I required for my new project and intended to read through after dinner. Someone had been tidying up while I was away, however, so that it took me a lot longer than I expected to locate precisely what it was I wanted and I was still there burrowing at it at seven o'clock – I heard the bell strike in the Ruggles Library tower. Judging that that was that for the moment, I readied to leave and was stuffing the documents I had unearthed into the diminutive carpetbag that I had brought with me so many years before from Paris, and that served me as a briefcase, when the sound of lone and echo-y footsteps along the corridor just outside my office caused me momentarily to arrest my movement. Everyone, I assumed, had gone home, and I suppose I was still affected by the very tangible aura of nervousness that I had left behind me in New Harbor ten days earlier.

The footsteps abruptly fell silent, there was a pause, then a tap at my door, on whose frosted glass a tall shadow hulked, and before I had time to say 'Come in,' Ralph MacMahon walked into the room.

I hadn't seen him since the afternoon we discovered Astrid together. He struck me now as paler and thinner, thinner at least in the face since the body was still deep and indecipherable inside its Michelin Man windbreaker. For about ten seconds he and I stood thus, directly opposite each other, I expectant and slightly puzzled, he quite inscrutable; until he said, as if we had already dispensed with all the usual formalities, 'You've been away.'

Since I couldn't think of anything else to remark I simply replied, 'Yes. I took time off. It was all too much for me, I'm afraid.'

Ralph mumbled something I didn't quite catch then asked whether I minded if he took a seat. I didn't, and he did. This was the excuse for another protracted silence, while I noted, with an uneasy memory of something else beginning to rise within me, that he was apparently determined to keep on his black leather gloves.

At last I decided to reassert my position. I told him I had been at that very instant about to leave for home and asked him rather shortly, I fear, to come to whatever point it was that had brought him unannounced to my door. He showed no surprise at this change of tone and tactic and stared at me for another six or seven seconds.

'Do you know, Professor Sfax,' he finally said, 'they still haven't found a clue to the murder – to either murder.'

I did know, having just rung Brophy, and I told Ralph so.

He took this, as they say, calmly 'on board.' 'Uh huh. But I think *I* have,' he said. 'You see, I've been doing some thinking myself – about Astrid's murder and Gillie's.'

'Gillie?' I queried, although I knew perfectly well whom he meant. It wasn't exclusively among the students that that had been Gillingwater's nickname.

'Gillingwater. I've thought about both of them, you know?' (I had already noticed in class that Ralph was one of those afflicted by the funny new American tic of turning statements into questions.) 'One after the other. Bang bang – just like that.'

I reminded him pedantically that neither of them had been shot and immediately felt that that had been a foolish thing to say. For, in a sense, as I told myself, Ralph and I had been soldered and seared together by the unforgettable revelation of Astrid's corpse; perhaps I owed it to him to indulge this final caprice.

'Maybe,' I said, 'you have a theory?'

'I do have a theory,' he replied with more animation than he had shown up to that point. 'Your theory.'

'Mine?'

'*The* Theory.'

'Ah,' I said wearily, in almost a sigh. 'And well, what about it?'

'Just that it occurred to me how it could be applied to these two murders.'

'Listen, Ralph,' I said, 'it's after seven and I'm exhausted. I returned very late last night, you know. Could we –'

'No,' he answered me categorically. 'It's important that you hear me out.'

Rather taken aback, I waited as patiently as I could for him to speak again, but there was yet another pause before he did.

'Now,' he began again, 'you would agree that there was no mystery to Astrid's death. She was murdered because she discovered some clue to why Gillingwater had been murdered, right?'

'I suppose so – right.'

'But the problem with Gillingwater, on the other hand, was that there wasn't any reason to kill *him*. I mean, even his students could have told you there was nothing there to commit murder for.'

'Yes, it's true.'

'Well then, what I started to think about was that whole metaphysics of presence thing, you know? The idea that there's really an absence where we all used to believe there was a presence?'

'For the sake of the argument – yes.'

'And it suddenly hit me that maybe the *absence* of a motive in murdering Gillingwater was in actual fact the *presence* of a motive.'

'I don't know that I follow you,' I said, even if something had occurred to me which made my speech for the moment a little thick.

Ralph looked hard at me. 'Everybody at the time said the same thing: that there was absolutely no reason for killing Gillingwater. Well, but what if he was murdered *because* there was no reason to murder him? What if the absence of a motivation *was* the motivation?'

Finding no reply to this, I let him continue.

'Well then, having gotten that far,' he said, 'I remembered another part of the Theory – you know, the either/or, the reversal of binary oppositions, what comes first but really shouldn't and what's the really significant factor, all of that?'

'I have to say I barely recognize it in that little thumbnail sketch, but go on.'

'Here were two murders, then, consecutive murders, one following the other just as one sentence follows another. Gillingwater is murdered first, we still don't know why, and Astrid is murdered second – why? Because she found out why Gillingwater had been murdered. But since we don't know what it was that she found out, the result's a vicious circle, right?'

'Right.'

'And so then I thought: What if the order is reversed? What if Astrid's was really the *first* murder?'

'What on earth do you mean, the first murder? You and I found Astrid's body more than a week after Gillingwater was killed. For Heaven's sake, the poor man had already been buried.'

'You surprise me, Professor,' he said with a sudden, unexpectedly cunning, teasing smile. 'I didn't expect *you* of all people to be so literal-minded.'

I stared at him as, without removing his gloves, he drew a crumpled pack of cigarettes from the pocket of his jeans and lit one with a heavy onyx lighter that sat on my desk.

'Let's construct a hypothesis,' he went on, and insolently exhaled a fine jet of smoke just above my head. 'Someone has his own good reasons for wanting Astrid Hunneker out of the way. But he realizes that, if he does murder her, the first thing the cops will go looking for is a motive – which is obviously something he has. So he's got to make it look as though there might have been *another* motive for killing her. And since he evidently knows her, and so must also know how mad she is for murder mysteries, he decides to commit another murder, a *second* murder first, a deliberately motiveless murder, an impossible, perfect crime. Then, when she rises to the bait exactly as he hoped she would, he dangles some phony, fabricated clue in front of her, the clue that will provide the *new* motive – and he kills her.'

I met his eyes in the silence that succeeded this exposition, but they were as unstartled, as carefully unnerved, by my scrutiny as a blind man's would be, and like a blind man's unfocused gaze made me feel almost as if I weren't there at all.

'That *is* a theory, Ralph,' I conceded at last, 'and rather a more ingenious and beautiful one in its way than *the* Theory. But where, I wonder, did it lead you?'

'To your door – unannounced,' he added mockingly.

'To *my* door ?'

'Professor, just two people, as I see it, could have had any motive for killing Astrid – and I know I didn't kill her.'

It was now my turn to pause before speaking again. 'Your innocence – if indeed it be the case – scarcely constitutes proof of my guilt.'

Ralph appeared to be sizing me up prior to the kill, grinning at me as invitingly, as encouragingly, as if he somehow trusted that my blunder would come to me before it had to be gross'y spelt out, grinning the way Tito used to grin before he would checkmate my king.

'Professor, I've known how to hack into computers since I was ten years old, and your Apple Mac was child's play. You really should have erased the evidence before going away, you know?'

Because? Because?

I found it in myself at last to ask him what he planned to do with his theory and I glanced over at the computer on the table in front of my office window. 'Are you going to Brophy? With that? It will certainly arouse suspicions, and it's damning enough to ruin me forever, but still, there's no proof in it that I killed Astrid.'

He stubbed the still smoking tip of his cigarette between his gloved thumb and forefinger and deposited the butt not, as I couldn't help remarking, in the glass ashtray on my desk but in his own pocket.

'Oh, Professor Sfax,' he said, 'once more you've misunderstood me. I have absolutely no intention of turning you in. No, no, this is where I mean to apply yet another part of the Theory.'

'Another part? What part?'

'The death of the Author.'

He unzipped some deep pocket of his windbreaker and took out a small and shiny automatic pistol, which he started to rotate about his gloved fingers while he went on speaking. 'It's called a Saturday night special – as easy to buy over the counter as a pack of condoms. You could have bought one with as little fuss as I did.'

'Ah, if you think you can kill me –' I started to say.

'Why should I kill you when you're about to kill yourself? You have so much on your conscience, after all. And as it wouldn't be right for you to die without squaring things, without first confessing to your crimes, you're going to write a touching little suicide note to explain that you couldn't bear to live on with the knowledge of everything you've done.'

'That is a grotesque proposal. I won't write a thing and you can't force me to.'

'I won't even try,' he said unpleasantly.

Still holding the pistol, which in an imperceptible fashion he had meanwhile transferred from his right hand to his left and into a position where, I could now observe, it was pointed directly at me, he tilted his chair over to my computer and switched it on.

'Here,' he said, 'on your Apple Mac, is where

your suicide note – or rather, Hermes' suicide note – is going to be written. It will make a nice postscript to all those fascinating confessions of yours. And since there won't be any question of handwriting I'll compose it for you if you like – posthumously.' He turned back to confront me, the pistol aimed now in my direction, unequivocally. 'What is it they say? An Apple a day keeps the doctor away. Say "aaah," Professor.'

I stared at him.

'What moronic game is this?'

He held the gun at his full arm's length, between my eyes. 'Say "aaah,"' he repeated, 'just as if you were at the doctor.'

I forced my mouth open. With an energy that I could not have predicted from his habitually lumbering gait he leaped up from the chair, leaned over my desk, and inserted the pistol's barrel into my throat. So close was his face to mine I could smell the bright white peppermint aroma of his toothpaste. Then he pulled the trigger.

....

Ralph's apprehension and arrest followed my death by no more than a matter of days. He had indeed typed into my computer an account and explanation of the whole squalid affair along with, on my supposed part, three or four pithy paragraphs of regret and propitiation. This he contrived to do, slowly, laboriously, without removing his gloves, which of course he was still wearing when he placed his pistol into my inert right hand. He left no fingerprints and no one had seen him either arrive or go.

Yet, like every murderer, so at least every great fictional detective has assured us, he made one fatal error. It was, as it happens, in the very matter of my style. He proved to be so utterly incompetent a pasticheur of its, shall I say, pseudo-Jamesian embonpoint that, to even an admirer of that style as gauche and unlettered as Brophy was, the 'join' was instantly visible. Even had I been at the end of my tether, even genuinely about to kill myself, Brophy felt quite properly that I would not, that I could not, have written the indifferently worded sentences which the screen appeared to impute to me.

As for my reputation, the jury is still, amazingly, out. It has taken a hard knock, to be sure, and possibly a mortal one, for the Theory's arch-enemies and a few of its former friends at once denounced the revelations (the 'Apple Mac texts,' as they became known, were eventually brought out in a single volume, entitled *The Death of the Author*, by the New Harbor Press) as quite the most damning indictment conceivable of the evil irrationalism that it and I had let loose upon the academic world. And that same pushy young man who had once accosted me on my own doorstep wrote a jocular piece in the *Village Voice* in which he wittily remarked that while one linguistic predicament might be regarded as a misfortune, two seemed like carelessness.

And yet. And yet already I detect the first faint timorous stirrings of revisionism and rehabilitation; my disciples, I feel sure, will be disinclined to stay for long on the defensive; a supposition just confirmed, indeed, by a lengthy essay, 'Léopold Sfax Is Not Who You Think He Is,' written by Francis-Xavier Pallette, Merkel Professor of Diacritical Studies at Breen, and published in the latest issue of *Semiotext(e)*.

As I could certainly have predicted of so vigorous and committed a convert to the Theory, Pallette has taken a strictly orthodox line on the case. He argues, notably, that there can be no history outside of these texts, no historical referent beyond the Apple Mac itself, inside which they are, as he admirably phrases it, 'hermetically immured,' and cites in illustration of their aporetic 'undecidability' the extreme ambiguity and incoherence of their temporal continuum. The very fact, as he points out, that 'Sfax' (whom he correctly treats throughout as a textual construct, not as any living individual) is assumed to have typed the texts on a word processor, precisely that Apple Mac that has given them their name, would appear to render wholly impossible, in terms at least of narrative verisimilitude or historical 'truth,' the climactic confrontation with MacMahon. 'What?' – Pallette sneeringly inquires of those who, with all their misgivings as to a certain disturbing inextricability of truth and untruth in the first two sections in particular, were in the end persuaded that the so-called Apple Mac texts could nevertheless be read as a reliable account of events that did actually occur outside of the computer – 'Did Sfax somehow manage to keep typing right up to the moment when the trigger was pulled?'

He also cleverly demonstrates just what little sense, when subjected to close critical scrutiny, many of the images used by 'Sfax' actually make: that repeated metaphor, for example, of the hare-and-tortoise pursuit around his watch face – 'the hour and minute hands of a watch,' Pallette reminds us, 'neither start nor end at the same place and therefore can scarcely be said to be racing one another' – or that other simile, charming and amusing enough in its way, of 'Sfax''s 'left forefinger serving as not much more than the right's assistant, intervening, like the less agile half of a tennis doubles partnership, to bag an occasional comma or apostrophe' – 'on computer keyboards,' again according to Pallette, 'commas and apostrophes are invariably in the catchment area of the right not the left forefinger.'

Oh, he has chopped me into little pieces; and I already sense that others are eager to follow his example and rally to my cause.

So here it is at last, the distinguished thing; here we two together are, on the very last page, the usually missing last page, of life's mystery story. And the truth, as you can see, is that this page is exactly like those which preceded it, except that the number of characters is already thinning out and the grain of the paper is just beginning to show through.

Have I any posthumous last words? Not really. As I have discovered to my disappointment, death *is* merely the displaced name for a linguistic predicament, and I rather feel like asking for my money back – as perhaps you do too, Reader, on closing this mendacious and mischievous and meaningless book.

A Selected List of Fiction Available from Minerva

While every effort is made to keep prices low, it is sometimes necessary to increase prices at short notice. Mandarin Paperbacks reserves the right to show new retail prices on covers which may differ from those previously advertised in the text or elsewhere.

The prices shown below were correct at the time of going to press.

	ISBN	Title	Author	Price
☐	7493 9145 6	**Love and Death on Long Island**	Gilbert Adair	£4.99
☐	7493 9130 8	**The War of Don Emmanuel's Nether Parts**	Louis de Bernieres	£5.99
☐	7493 9903 1	**Dirty Faxes**	Andrew Davies	£4.99
☐	7493 9056 5	**Nothing Natural**	Jenny Diski	£4.99
☐	7493 9173 1	**The Trick is to Keep Breathing**	Janice Galloway	£4.99
☐	7493 9124 3	**Honour Thy Father**	Lesley Glaister	£4.99
☐	7493 9918 X	**Richard's Feet**	Carey Harrison	£6.99
☐	7493 9028 X	**Not Not While the Giro**	James Kelman	£4.99
☐	7493 9112 X	**Hopeful Monsters**	Nicholas Mosley	£6.99
☐	7493 9029 8	**Head to Toe**	Joe Orton	£4.99
☐	7493 9117 0	**The Good Republic**	William Palmer	£5.99
☐	7493 9162 6	**Four Bare Legs in a Bed**	Helen Simpson	£4.99
☐	7493 9134 0	**Rebuilding Coventry**	Sue Townsend	£4.99
☐	7493 9151 0	**Boating for Beginners**	Jeanette Winterson	£4.99
☐	7493 9915 5	**Cyrus Cyrus**	Adam Zameenzad	£7.99

All these books are available at your bookshop or newsagent, or can be ordered direct from the publisher. Just tick the titles you want and fill in the form below.

Mandarin Paperbacks, Cash Sales Department, PO Box 11, Falmouth, Cornwall TR10 9EN.

Please send cheque or postal order, no currency, for purchase price quoted and allow the following for postage and packing:

UK including BFPO	£1.00 for the first book, 50p for the second and 30p for each additional book ordered to a maximum charge of £3.00.
Overseas including Eire	£2 for the first book, £1.00 for the second and 50p for each additional book thereafter.

NAME (Block letters) ....

ADDRESS ....

....

☐ I enclose my remittance for ....

☐ I wish to pay by Access/Visa Card Number ☐☐☐☐☐☐☐☐☐☐☐☐☐☐☐☐

Expiry Date ☐☐☐☐